Maxim Jakubowski

is a former publisher and owner of the world-famous Murder One bookshop in London's Charing Cross Road. As well as being a writer and editor of various cult publishing imprints, he is acknowledged as a disturbing and controversial voice in contemporary fiction. His collections have sold massively, he is a regular on TV and radio where he is an expert on crime, erotica and film, and a Guardian columnist. He is literary director of the prestigious CRIME SCENE festival held at London's NFT in July.

First Published in Great Britain in 2002 by
The Do-Not Press Limited
16 The Woodlands
London SE13 6TY
www.thedonotpress.co.uk
email: kms@thedonotpress.co.uk

Casebound edition: ISBN 1 899 344 88 8
B-format paperback: ISBN 1 899344 87 X

British Library Cataloguing in Publication Data. A catalogue
record for this book is available from the British Library.

1   3   5   7   9   10   8   6   4   2

Printed and bound in Great Britain by
The Guernsey Press Co Ltd.

KISS ME SADLY

by
Maxim Jakubowski

– to Jim Driver and Franck Spengler, who believed.

– to all those, past and present, who accepted me for what I am.

Also by Maxim Jakubowski published by The Do-Not Press:

It's You That I Want To Kiss
Because She Thought She Loved Me
On Tenderness Express
The State of Montana
The Erotic Novels Boxed Set

1

She said pussy.

I said cunt.

Just a minor misunderstanding in our confused exploration of the world of lust.

Sexual semantics the way Brits and Americans differ on their pronunciation of the word 'tomato' maybe?

For her, pussy was playful, gently sexy, fond as well as provocative, almost an endearment.

To me, it just sounded downright vulgar. A word used too often in bad X-rated movies with inane and damn inappropriate canned muzak on the soundtrack to accompany the vaginal hydraulics on open display, or whatever other orifice the action chose to feature in intimate close-up. A very American word.

Maybe she'd had too many American correspondents or cybersex partners on the Internet.

Pussy just reminded me of cats. I hated cats.

In her opinion, cunt was too direct, too offensive, too raw.

For me, it was something natural, honest, and a matter-of-fact word to describe the female sex, a body part which never failed to fascinate and obsess me. I was naturally aware that there were a further hundred or more names for it, descriptions and euphemisms and such. I even had a book on my shelves which gloriously listed them all, with origin, language and etymology analysed in cod scholarly fashion. Don't ever fault my research.

I did not believe in fancy words that skirted the subject: a cunt was a cunt was a cunt.

And each successive one I encountered was so blissfully different, a brand new experience, a source of wonder and delight, shapes, colours, shades, odour, variations, taste, texture, all worthy of a thousand narratives. There was little need for words to map a woman's sex as far as I was concerned. Just too many words to describe it that confused the issue.

Don't get me wrong: some men are born tit men, leg fetishists or arse lovers; and, for me, the eyes and the face were always the first features to catch my attention in a woman. Cunt, of course, came later. Or in many cases never, as my relationship didn't always necessarily carry me so far.

It was a body part you graduated to with honours in your rite of seduction. A supreme reward and thus unique. Private. Shockingly incomparable.

So, imagine my surprise when, towards the end of a routine e-mail one day in late spring, Milduta wrote me that she had just shaved her pussy.

Three weeks earlier we had been in New York, staying together at a small hotel on the borders of Greenwich Village. We had spent almost a week there, her first ever visit to Manhattan, and between feverish bouts of fucking, had walked miles, browsing shops, me gleefully buying her clothes and silk thongs from Victoria's Secret, eating too much Japanese food, seeing movies, visiting museums, hunting down bars where they served fresh carrot juice which she could down by the gallon, discovering to our mutual surprise how well we fitted together sexually and emotionally. During our sex games I had often trimmed her, taking voyeuristic pleasure in thinning her pubes so that her meaty gash was openly revealed in its full glory behind the protective curtain of her curls. I had, almost jokingly, suggested not for the first time she shave her genital area. She had declined with a knowing smile, yet again pretexting the discomfort of the hair growing back afterwards and how her skin often reacted with undue irritation and unseemly pimples. She'd had experience of this when she had briefly lived with a Swiss banker in Zurich. A dominant personality, he had required her to be shaven below. She had, initially, obligingly played along with his desires, still at a stage when she was testing the nascent relationship, unsure whether it held the prospect of becoming a permanent one.

With a laugh, she had also revealed that the banker shaved around his cock and balls, so that their smoothness had matched. An image that often fanned my erotic imagination.

My first reaction when I read her mail was to guess she had met another man.

Surely, when a woman reveals her intimacy so openly, it is for a man. Why him and not me? But she assured me she had only done it on a whim. Waxing her bikini line in the bathroom one morning, she had miscalculated and depilated unevenly. Getting rid of the rest was just a way of putting things right, she said. And it felt so sexy, she added. Not like in Switzerland where it was part of sexual compact. Now it was just for herself and no one else. She felt so naked below when riding her bike to the nearby town where she did her food shopping, and arousal came so easy in the knowledge of the secret she harboured down there. She sounded both amused and amazed that it should be so. I could have told her that long before, my fascination for smooth pudenda having steadily progressed from airbrushed models on pornographic playing cards to hardcore movies and evocative nude photography.

I wondered when I saw Milduta again what the effect on my libido would be to witness her naked cunt without its curtain of soft, darker curls. The only women I had ever known with smooth vaginas had been so from the outset of our affairs. Would knowing the 'before' and the 'after' of a woman's genitals have the same erotic effect on me? A thought that nagged me for weeks to come.

I wrote back, asking her to stay shaven until we could find the opportunity to meet up again.

'I'm not sure,' she answered.

It was that hesitancy that triggered my suspicions and the fear soon gripped me of losing Milduta, that I would never rest my eyes on the wonderful vision of her cunt in all its splendid and utter nudity.

I'd always known our relationship was far from exclusive. There was no way it could ever be, due to our personal circumstances.

<... oh, u know, I just shave my pussy... lol... is feel so sexy...>

Well, she certainly chose her moment, didn't she?

2

Life is not a movie.

The choices are always far from clear cut. The villains walk in various shades of grey and the solutions to problems are complicated as hell.

Actually, films make it all look too easy and their subtle art of deception warps the mind, soon beginning to affect your actions in most insidious ways. You are not a character in someone else's plot, and there is no certainty of three acts and a happy-ever-after ending. You have no control of the situations, whether good or bad.

Life is a mess and makes no sense and often feels like an accumulation of clichés; at any rate, that's the way it looks if you consider the whole thing with some degree of cynicism (some might actually say realism). So it is no sin to accept the ambiguous romanticism and peacefulness of the images flickering on the screen, because you aspire to goodness, to happiness, and the conscious retreat into daydream or fantasy is such an easy road to follow.

Life made easy.

So...

It begins like a movie. With a wide screen and a sumptuous wash of music, massed strings – or more likely synthesiser chords in this day and age of budget consciousness – eventually rising to a majestic crescendo. Random images coalesce and a melancholy sort of melody emerges from the unformed wall of sound... 'Porcelain' by Moby maybe, or the sad tones of Nico as orchestrated by John Cale, like the soundtrack for an imaginary western, the climax of which might prove particularly bittersweet: a gunfight, lovers parted by fate, hearts asunder, a desert, a ravine, a tear.

It's a tune that aims straight for the heart but hints at further sadness to come, further down the highway. Sadness, yes; because tragedy is much too strong a word and the world we live in is so full of incomplete people, with small hopes and minuscule epiphanies that pale against the true suffering that always seems to occur elsewhere in the lives and countries of others. Some might even state that there are no tragedies for people like you and me, just minor inconveniences.

The credits of the movie roll at last, rising from the heart of the music, and indistinct shapes emerge out of the blurry chaos that occupies the screen and its rectangular geometry. Panavision format, just like in the good old days.

A woman's voice is heard, plaintive, across the gradually fading sounds of the poignant music.

Is she singing? Crying? Sighing?

Has she a quaint, breathless and somewhat exotic foreign accent to your practised ears?

A voice that evokes longing.

To which you invariably respond with open heart. Lowering your defences. Revealing your fundamental vulnerability.

Fool that you are.

3

Jack had struck lucky with the dotcom boom.

As an inveterate book collector, he had never been particularly interested in technological developments, even if his interest in science fiction went back to his childhood and he knew his Arthur C Clarke from his Philip K. Dick and his William Gibson and appreciated the subtle difference between steampunk and cyberpunk, hard science SF and space opera. Actually, he had almost moved straight from manual typewriter to computer word processing, with barely a couple of years working with an electric typewriter, because of his natural reluctance to accept change.

He found computers to be alien and unwieldy but his collection was growing out of control and he had to somehow come up with a system to catalogue his considerable holdings of books and old magazines, let alone the ongoing new publications that flooded his mail box on a daily basis since he had been reviewing the stuff in a weekly magazine.

He had used filing cards but the system wasn't working and proved impractical when it came to cross-referencing short stories in anthologies and magazines for easy reference.

He'd asked around and found that most other collectors suffered from similar drawbacks.

In the absence of anything on the bibliophile market that could respond to his needs, he tried, by trial and error and conspicuous consumption of unreadable manuals, to devise a software programme that would work on his domesticated

Apple and somehow tame the database beast to his finicky satisfaction.

Much to his surprise, a year or so later a random conversation at a book publication party at the Groucho with an executive from a newly launched Internet sales company led to an expression of interest in the system he had cobbled together and, six months later, he pocketed a large cheque which, for the first time in his life, afforded him a life of gentle financial ease. He left his job as Export Director (Europe and Africa) for a middle-sized American food raw materials and ingredients group, and abandoned a rat race he had never truly enjoyed.

He decided to stick to what he knew best and opened a small bookshop.

This gave him more leisure time to read, grow his CD collection to book-like proportions, research, travel America several times a year, scouring old and dust-ridden second-hand book emporiums for further gems and curios for his personal shelves and, of course, the store. A life he would only have dreamed of ten or fifteen years earlier. But the lack of urgency and the reassuring financial stability soon alerted him to the level of raging dissatisfaction brewing inside him. He'd divorced some years before, amiably. There were no children so no one had really been hurt. His fault, of course. A wandering eye, too many opportunities in hotel lounges and bars during his export travel days and nights.

He missed marriage.

Hated being alone. Knew that it brought out the worst in him.

Lust. Laziness. And an overflow of tenderness.

Like all men with talent, Jack had many flaws. He was realistically aware of the fact and often listed them distractedly against the screen of his mind as he tried to reach the refuge of sleep. But the worse trait was how he romanticised over women time and time again, never somehow learning from his experiences. A problem that annoyed the efficient businessmen in him like hell. But this perception of his shortcomings didn't mean he could change the way he acted and felt when a particular woman came across his path and had his chords and other attributes twitching...

He knew all too well how the emotions women created inside his head and body invariably skewed his perception of them and coloured all his relationships.

Recognising this and knowing the existence of this fatal Achilles heel still could not prevent him from making the same old mistakes over and over again.

Was it the way he had been brought up?

The fact that his father never had the guts, or the time, to tell him about the birds and the bees? Or treated him like an alien form he couldn't really understand, this little boy with dark curly hair and repressed feelings, always with his nose inside books or his sports magazines and with little interest in the activities his father could approve of?

This child who, silently, furtive like no other, would mentally store and interpret all the distorted facts about the way men and women coexist and war from telltale stories circulating amongst school kids, or accept as gospel the fantasies of life provided by the wide-screen Cinemascope Hollywood romantic comedies he would invariably watch on his weekly Thursday afternoon outings to the local cinema.

He often tried to puzzle out how this fundamental flaw at the heart of his being had come to be.

Education? Family life? The lies of films and fiction? A particular woman? But which: the first girl he had coveted from afar? The first he had kissed? The first he had slept with? The first who had dropped him?

Or, more likely, the first young woman who savagely, unknowingly wounded him, his emotions scarred by her betrayal, the first he had felt longings for.

Yes, that was more likely, he knew.

London. His final year in high school. A large, high-ceilinged room in a meandering South Kensington flat and a dozen or so teenagers sitting in a circle on the parquet floor.

Sometimes, Jack would wonder whether his recent life would have been any different had he remained in his marriage, managed to salvage it from his mistakes and his wife had produced children. Would it have tamed his emptiness or made it even worse? Pure speculation, though, as two successive ectopic pregnancies had put paid to that possibility just three years into the marriage, adding sorrow to the sadness of his failure to make the relationship work.

He was not unattractive, he knew, in a rugged and intellectual sort of way. 'Your looks always remind me of a wild and impetuous Hungarian pianist,' a close woman friend, not in his sexual circle, had once told him. This had amused him mightily. Better than being compared to Mel Brooks or Charles Aznavour, as had also happened once, much to his puzzlement and irritation.

When women he chatted with online asked him to describe himself, he invariably would inform them that he was neither Brad Pitt nor Frankenstein, before supplying the tiresome and customary statistics. None ever queried whether he was referring to the sad Baron or the eponymous monster he had unwittingly created.

The joke served him well quite often.

4

Milduta's presence in the world of men had nagged her from early teenage years onwards.

Her father left home when she was only two and she had few memories of him. She had been brought up by her mother, with much assistance from her grandparents in whose house they both lived until she reached the age of nine, together with her brother who was five years older than she was and already moved within his own circle of friends. It was then that her mother had met Piotr and married again. Her new stepfather worked in one of the ministries and already had two children of his own from a failed marriage where his previous wife had just decamped to the West one day, abandoning her family in her wake. There was just not enough room in his flat for Milduta and her brother, so it was agreed they would remain with the grandparents until her mother and Piotr could afford a larger place. It never happened. Within two years of her remarriage, their mother fell ill one harsh winter and never recovered. To Milduta's grandparents' relief, Piotr declined to take them in following the funeral and steps were officially taken for the older couple to adopt the two children. Estonia had never been a very sentimental place.

Regardless, her childhood was a happy one. She was an easy, undemanding child, who kept herself happy with just a few old toys for company, and could occupy her time on the kitchen floor with a battery of saucepan lids and a spoon or two. Her brother, on the other hand, was a problem kid who left school early to apprentice as a plumber and would later become a notorious drunkard and adulterer. They had little in common.

Milduta was studious, made friends easily with other girls at school, but remained shy in the presence of boys. They didn't scare her or bully her; they were just alien to her little world and, until she reached twelve, she paid little attention to them and found no necessity to consort with them in the school's playground or join in their games in the street outside her grandparents' house.

There had been a commotion in the neighbourhood. Adults were restless.

Milduta had been allowed to stay over one Saturday night at a nearby school friend's house.

'Everyone is so touchy,' Aida had told her.

'Why?' Milduta had queried.

'Haven't you heard?' her friend asked.

'What?'

Her friend stirred on the other side of the bed they shared and turned closer to Milduta.

'That girl from class 6, I think her name is Rosa, you know, the tall and skinny one who always wears her hair plaited?'

'Yes, I see her around,' Milduta replied. It was a lanky girl from the class four years above them. She had always struck Milduta as particularly pretty.

'She's been found dead. Murdered.'

'What?'

Aida cuddled up to her in the darkness and lowered her voice.

'They say she was raped.'

'No!'

'And strangled.'

'Really?'

'It was near the docks. They say the police have no idea who did it.'

The two young girls shivered and held hands under the thick, rough, wool blanket.

As the night lengthened, their conversation turned to whispers and the more worldly Aida spun wild speculations around the case of the murdered schoolgirl.

At first, Milduta had assumed rape was just another way of killing people, until her friend actually explained the act to her, raising in her mind a mad welter of confusion and terrible curiosity.

She had, on a few rare occasions, caught her grandfather or older brother naked when either had forgotten to close the bathroom door whilst taking a shower. Somehow she had never given too much attention to their genitals. They were different, that was all it was. Her curiosity had been minimal.

Rosa's murder was never solved that she remembered, but the memory stayed burning bright in young Milduta's mind and never again did she recapture her innocence. Now she knew what men were capable of, what their cocks could do. And the Pandora's box of her imagination had been pried open and could never be closed again.

For months, she shamefully pictured the rape in her mind, in all its gory details (Aida had had to give her detailed lessons in amatory anatomy since her grandparents had always shied away from the subject) and shamefully found herself not only immensely curious but also strangely aroused by the idea of a man mounting a woman thus, forcing her open and tearing her with his brute strength. Soon, she was imagining this happening to her, in the penumbra of the dockyards or the twilight of the sparse forest that bordered the edge of town. She knew it was wrong, but when half sleep came at night, muted sounds from the television her grandparents watched in the other room filtering through the thin partition, and the horrible thoughts would flood all over her again and again. The man abusing her never had a face, or even a particular body shape; all she could conjure up in her feverish thoughts was a monstrous penis of abominable size and savage mien (she had just encountered, through another girlfriend, her first Japanese erotic prints in an art book from the adult section of the public library, and blissfully assumed that men's cocks in full bloom genuinely reached such gargantuan proportions).

From that time onward, men and their attributes began to fascinate and attract her. Not that schoolboys of her own age held the least attraction. Somehow, they didn't seem to qualify for manhood. Just insignificant kids who would never grow up and attain that quality of fear she instinctively sought in the opposite sex.

Real men surely were creatures of another ilk, with powers that eluded her. Men who would tame her, take her, rape her, dominate her, give her life a meaning. They were different.

This became Milduta's secret life.

She slowly blossomed. Acquired more social graces, widened her friendships in and out of school with those of her own age, consigned her teddy bears to her bedroom shelf and no longer played with them.

She became a fun person to be with, accepted as such by the varied groups she wove in and out of, at school, at play, mingling with her older brother's friends when she had to. Always rough and ready for a game, a challenge, a tumble. They treated her as an equal, a familiar and easygoing tomboy. This suited Milduta well as she almost scientifically studied them, these boys who were not quite men, with amused detachment, learning piece by piece the complex jigsaw that was the world of men, the other side.

Her breasts came late and were never quite as opulent as Aida's and most of her girlfriends. She would eventually grow into a B-cup, barely. But from the moments those bumps made their bow inside her blue school shirt and her grandmother took her shopping for her first bra, she noticed with fascination how the young men she had played rough games with, the older men in the street or in shops, seemed to look at her in a new way.

Thus did Milduta discover lust.

5

Catherine Guinard was not the prettiest young girl in his philosophy class during Jack's first year in a mixed school. Nowhere near; red-haired Rhoona DeMole, voluptuous Beatrice, slinky Elizabeth and Jacqueline, who would later become a minor movie starlet, ruled that roost by far. But something about her touched him inside in insidious ways, where it mattered.

Maybe that was Jack's fundamental flaw: he thought with his emotions, not with his cock.

Or, still recovering from his mother's premature death, he didn't realise how his vulnerability showed.

Catherine was small in height and in proportions, had thin, mousey, light brown hair, which fell in a forlorn fringe on her round forehead. She also sported slightly crooked, albeit shimmering, white teeth. She came from the French provinces and dressed anonymously, with a liking for skirts with Burberry patterns and knee-high black leather boots. Whenever she was not with friends, she would wear glasses to read and work.

But you know how it is: it's never just the way women look that does it; it's the way they laugh, or how their eyes sparkle at a given moment, the shape of the curl of an upper lips, or a special way of sighing and expressing a longing, a sadness. There is no magic formula. It's a thing they do as if to the manor born. The invisible art of seduction, which invariably seems to catch one lost soul in their tender nets without a woman even making much of an effort, let alone designating a sentimental target.

For several months, Jack worshipped Catherine from afar.

They never ventured out together alone, but always as part of a larger group of schoolmates. Communal revision time below the wooden shelves of the French Institute; walks during the lunch break in the rooms of the Natural History Museum or, when the weather grew milder, in its gardens; sipping tepid beer and playing darts in the nearby pubs, which the French students spending a year in London absolutely adored; or large, boisterous outings to the few art cinemas in London that screened films with subtitles. They were just part of the crowd.

Later, he offered to help her with homework and projects.

Sitting at a table at her lodgings off Ladbroke Grove, smelling her fragrance as she assiduously noted his suggestions, drowning in her quiet presence. It was a new experience, overwhelming, strange.

'So, next week, if you want, we can go over Schopenhauer?'

'That's so nice of you. I just have a problem sorting out all these German theories, you know. Maybe something about being French and living in England. I can only fathom one new culture at a time. You're very kind.'

'It's nothing, Catherine. I'm just happy to help.'

But more often than not, Jack remained speechless when it came to important matters.

It was a Saturday night. That afternoon, a whole group of students from the philosophy class had ventured into the West End to see a Sophia Loren movie in Leicester Square, a WWII film in which she played a mother whose daughter was ravished during the tumult of the invasion of Italy by American and Allied forces. They were all seventeen or, at most, eighteen. Some of the girls had shed a tear while the boys had remained eloquently silent during the course of the post-movie commentary. It was just about getting dark and someone suggested they all move on to Kensington and eat fish and chips. They opted for the labyrinthine building in which Catherine and three other visiting French students were all lodging individually.

Some drinks later, seven of them sat in a circle on the carpeted floor of Anita's bedroom, as hers was by chance the largest room in the house.

Catherine faced Jack, on the other side of the circle of adolescents.

Later, he wouldn't remember how the conversation had led to this point, or who had come up with the suggestion in the first place.

'We should have a game of truth,' someone suggested.

Some of them, including Jack, didn't know what it was all about.

'Haven't you seen Les Tricheurs?'

It had been a popular and fashionable film in France the year before, about spoiled, golden youth and their nascent love and misbehaviour. Jack had already been back in England at the time, and knew the film only by name and reputation.

The game had no doubt existed for many generations past, but the notoriety of the movie had propelled it back into fashion.

It was simple: each participant in the game would have to ask a question to a person of his or her choice in the circle and they would be obligated to answer truthfully.

'Or else?' Jack queried.

'It's a matter of honour,' one of the girls replied.

Without giving the matter much thought, Jack accepted the rules.

Someone dimmed the room's lights and Catherine fetched a couple of coloured candles from her own room and lit them with a giggle and no little sense of drama.

Jack knew most of those sitting around him reasonably well. He'd never spoken to the Scandinavian girl, Greta, before today but she seemed pleasant. She returned his smile when he glanced at her, sitting as she was across from him, on Catherine's immediate left.

The early questions were harmless. About favourite foods, when they had last been drunk, brutal opinions of their respective teachers.

'This is boring,' Pierre muttered, but everyone heard him.

He was not Jack's favourite amongst the group of friends. He was undoubtedly good-looking and was painfully aware of the fact; smug, always impeccably dressed, a scion from a rich French family from the provinces. His reasons for attending the school in London were anything but academic.

'So,' someone said, 'make it more interesting when it's your turn.'

Pierre smiled.

Two questions later (one about President de Gaulle and his popularity, and another about the moral dilemma of torture by French troops during the war in Algeria) it became Pierre's turn to challenge someone in the circle.

He looked straight towards Greta who, even in the rising darkness of the bedroom, visibly blushed. Everyone knew she fancied him.

'Greta?'

'Yes,' she replied in a whisper.

Theatrically, Pierre took his time. Finally, he asked her:

'Which man here do you like most?'

Someone sniggered.

The Swedish girl blushed even deeper.

'Come on, Gret,' another girl said. 'No lying.'

Greta lowered her eyes and finally mumbled the name of another boy who sat there, a shy young man from Montpellier whom everyone considered quite inoffensive.

Pierre protested.

'It's not true, Greta,' desperately trying to embarrass the girl who did not wish to reveal her attraction for him.

'I'm not,' she complained weakly. 'Julien is just a nice person. It doesn't mean that I have feelings for him,' she added. 'He's just a good friend.'

Julien himself had gone crimson, never one to enjoy being the centre of attention.

There was quiet laughter from some. They knew she had lied.

So, now, it was her turn to field a question.

Angered by what he had done to her, she confronted Pierre. 'Which of the girls in this room have you kissed?' she asked.

They all drew their breath. Things were getting serious now. For a brief moment, Jack considered what he might have answered had the question been flung at him. He would have had to lie to safeguard his pride. Naturally, he had kissed none of the young women here, least of all Catherine.

'That's a boring question, Greta. Didn't you rather want to ask which I have had sex with?'

She said nothing.

All eyes were on Pierre now. One of the other boys interjected. 'Come on, Pierre, you have to provide an answer'.

Finally, having carefully and ostentatiously weighed all the arguments for honesty or discretion, Pierre spat out a name.

None of them had somehow expected it. His room was across the landing from hers and it seems he had sweet-talked her into a fuck just a week before. No one even felt she was his type.

'Catherine.'

Jack's heart dropped a thousand vertical paces to the ground at this unexpected and devastating news. He didn't even notice Catherine swiftly rising from her crouch, tears streaming down her cheeks and running to her room. Anger? Shame?

Jack was stunned, felt pinned to the floor, unable to move.

The game petered out.

Later, he even heard Pierre boasting that Catherine wasn't that good in bed, too passive and all that.

It only made the turmoil worse inside his teenage heart.

6

Her erstwhile parents were anything but intellectuals; before he decamped (her mother first pretended he had romantically gone to work at sea, then later would just shrug her shoulders with feigned indifference; some years later, her brother told Milduta that he had once seen their father walking by in the street below their building, hand in hand with another woman and child – his new family – which certainly sounded like a more realistic fate to the teenagers), Milduta's enigmatic father had worked installing shower units and her mother was a functionary in a local government office dealing with pensions and benefits. But somehow, the ill-fated couple had both enjoyed a love of grand opera. Maybe that was how they had first met, she speculated. It was as good a theory as any other.

So, she was called Mimi, in homage to the melancholy heroine of La Bohème.

It had long puzzled Milduta.

No one in Estonia appeared to be called Mimi apart from her.

And she didn't like to stick out from the crowd. Like all children, she was a conformist at heart. It was safer.

'That's because you are so special,' her mother had said. 'Maybe one day you will become a singer and we will come and listen to you at the Opera House on opening night, wearing our best evening clothes, of course. What a day that will be; my daughter, the belle of the ball!'

But Mimi proved to have no special talent for music. In her first year in primary school, she was seduced into learning to play an instrument.

Of all those available, she insisted on choosing the accordion.

The only one available at the school was enormous, dwarfed her small frame when she practised, and spectators couldn't help smiling quietly when they witnessed her on stage playing the *Internationale* or some other obligatory, and easy-to-learn, folk tune at the traditional end-of-year concert by the pupils. She always had to wear a silly local peasant costume for the occasion, which made her ever so irritable. A right little madam, her teachers would say.

But she grew to like her name. After all, it got people interested in her. Questioning the origins of the name, drawing sighs of amazement from elder folk. Which is more than could be said for her brother, plain old Pavel, whose name was thirteen to the dozen and ever so common, as she would never tire of telling him when they argued.

After her mother's remarriage and desertion, her grandparents – who'd never quite understood why she was called Mimi – began calling her Milduta, a diminutive full of endearment, and that was how most people and friends soon came to know her as she grew older.

Many years later, it was only when she gazed at her passport, or her Party or identity card, that she remembered she was actually called Mimi, like that girl in the Italian opera who ended up badly.

The initial period in the sole care of her grandparents was particularly unhappy for Milduta. Even though she had never been particularly close to her mother, who devoted most of her time to a surfeit of socialising in an effort to rebuild her life rather than care for her children, Milduta found she missed her enormously. An occasional meal at her mother's new house at weekends, with their acquired stepfather glowering at them in disapproval, and his kids making faces at her, became a regular ordeal rather than the pleasure it should have been for her.

As kind and solicitous as her grandparents were, they were also old and smelled that way; their breath, their hair, the soap they used. And, inside, she knew she shouldn't feel that way. The guilt settled over her.

As unhappy days streamed by, Milduta would lie in her bed at night, listening to the silence invade the small attic room she had been consigned to and watched, bleary-eyed, as darkness took over. She would invariably remind herself that she was special.

'I am special,' like a soft whisper emerging from the grey, grubby quilt and the small shape buried within it.

Like a mantra.

Then she would finally manage to find sleep and would doze off with a beatific smile all over her face.

It was an expression that later almost became a permanent one.

Her smile became a wonder to behold.

Her lips always seemed to be smiling and her eyes sparkled likewise, even when she was not in the least happy.

But she was already growing into a teenager and that ever-present, amiable and almost childlike smile often conveyed totally the wrong impression.

To the opposite sex.

A smile of both innocence and total acceptance.

That was the one feature about Milduta that began attracting men to her like fireflies. A streak of submissiveness that spoke to them in silent words or emotions.

For many years, she was quite unaware of it.

7

So, Catherine Guinard became the first to carve a deep notch across his heartstrings.

Others would follow.

He'd returned home that night after the game, buried in a dense fog of pain, oblivious to his surroundings: the night streets of Ladbroke Grove, the Circle Line and its late-night drunks, cavernous Liverpool Street and the halting train to the Eastern suburbs where he lived. Sleep came late (it was already morning) as a relief. Fortunately, it was Sunday and he had no classes. He knew he couldn't face seeing Pierre or Catherine, or any of his Lycée friends, so quickly again.

But it was impossible to avoid them after a week or so and, her eyes lowered and hesitant, Catherine sought his assistance for an essay on Hegel.

He agreed.

'Why did you do it?' he finally asked after several hours of hesitation, while they sipped orange juice and concentrated on the work at hand.

Catherine answered quietly. She had been aware of his feelings for her before. It would have been impossible not to, what with his puppy-dog stance around her.

'I'm so sorry,' she answered.

She fell silent.

Jack failed to react.

'I'm sorry you had to learn about it that way,' she finally added.

'It was a shock,' Jack mumbled. Something of an under-statement.

'We live in the same house, Pierre is good-looking, I was feeling homesick that evening and he was nice to me, you know how it goes; we cuddled as friends and he sort of sweet-talked me into it. It was my first time.'

Jack swallowed hard.

'I do regret it now,' Catherine continued. 'I know that for him I'm just another conquest. He has no feelings for me...' She trailed off and looked down on the table at their papers again.

Jack guessed she was omitting something important.

He queried her.

'But you still have feelings for him, don't you?'

She sighed, 'I do, Jack. I know I shouldn't. He's vain, superficial and takes advantage of people when it suits him, but you can't rule your heart that easily, can you?'

Jack could feel the grey fog again settling down over his heart.

'And me?'

'What?'

'What do you feel about me?'

She looked up again.

'I like you, Jack, but as a friend. I don't think I could feel otherwise.'

He felt like pleading, justifying his unrequited affection, but he was too shy and felt he lacked the necessary eloquence.

'I see,' is all he managed to say in answer.

'I'm sorry, Jack,' she said again.

'It's OK.'

'We'll always be good friends. Can't we?' Catherine said.

'Of course,' Jack agreed.

But he knew that the concept of friendship between boy and girl, man and woman, once feelings had reared their ugly head, was a difficult one. A state of play he would seldom achieve in his future life. It was love or it was indifference. Friendship had no rewards.

They returned to the safer ground of philosophy essays and saw much less of each other during the following months.

At odd moments, during class, he would gaze in her direction as she sat, rapt in attention, but she seldom returned his look.

She remained outwardly friendly with Pierre, but he didn't know whether they had sex again. He guessed they did. The opportunities were there. Same house, same circle of friends.

One year later, when they had both moved back to France – Jack to study Comparative Literature at the Sorbonne, Catherine to attend a school of Advanced Administration in her home town of Boulogne – he called on Catherine, who was passing through Paris and staying with friends or family near the Rue Saint Sulpice. They had a coffee, said little of importance and never met or spoke again thereafter.

All these years later, he could barely remember what she looked like, just a vague memory of a small girl with sparrow-like features, a thin nose and a weak chin. Not even his type.

In the litany of sentimental hurt that punctuated his twenties, he invariably turned to blondes, whom he learned to approach with utmost caution, after the initial rebuffs or expressions of calculated indifference. But he learned to persevere.

Maybe, he reasoned, he wasn't good enough for blondes. Or they were too good for him. Some basic, chemical incompatibility between blondness and insecure Jewish men with dark hair and a modicum of brains? And sometimes, when he was between women, between loves – or at any rate between infatuations – he would look back at the peregrinations of his affections over the years and mentally juggle memories by attempting to balance his past sexual statistics by hair colour. An absurd form of list making.

The results never made sense actually.

Because sometimes the whim of women didn't follow any sense of logic either.

8

Men liked Milduta.

But as she learned how to deal with them, she soon came to the realisation that they wanted more of her than she was willing to give.

The boys of her age or thereabouts at school, or friends of her brothers who fancied their chances, were easy enough. They begged for a kiss, for a token of her affection. A peck on the cheek was deemed insufficient. They wanted her mouth, her tongue, against theirs but seldom more. The mere notion of sex or bodily intimacy was still beyond them, unthinkable, far across the horizon of their wildest, shy dreams. She knew that if she had allowed Bogdan to French-kiss her at the burger bar that Saturday, or Ivan to feel her breast through the fabric of her thick cardigan, even though he had grubby fingers, they both would have been nonplussed as to what further steps they might have ventured beyond. They were just kids, immature. Boys.

The men who would offer to buy her coffees or beers at the bar where many of her girlfriends and she would congregate were another kettle of fish altogether.

The lust in their eyes betrayed their baser instinct. For them, she was prey, a target for use and depredation. And, confronted with the readiness of Milduta's smile, they could not understand why she kept on rebuffing them.

But she was also fascinated by their persistence, the inner certainty some of them visibly had of their power, as if they knew that one day she would inevitably pass on to the other side, accept her place in their world. Because of the slut that lay dormant deep inside her. They knew that there was a slut in every young girl. A slut wetted by curiosity and hormonal progress.

Milduta also knew she was playing a dangerous game when it came to older men and their rampant desires.

So she went to bars after class and clubs at weekends, most often with the security of other girlfriends as part of a loud crowd, but also sometimes with just Aida when they would dress specifically to provoke. Short skirts, tight sweaters, knee-high boots. The best uniform to cadge free drinks.

She enjoyed the company of men, usually ten or so years older than she was. She would dance with them across the smokey floors of youth clubs or junior Party or pioneer social meetings. Kept them company as they downed endless glasses of vodka, which she could easily match.

There were rules. Aida, who was less touchy about the etiquette of exploiting men, taught her the basics. After three drinks they always insisted on some form of further contact: a slow dance, rubbing against her, or slapping her rump with their sweaty hands. She allowed it. It was harmless. She always knew when to stop, when to say no to further physical overtures.

In a curious way, she even invited their attentions. It was a matter of pride to her that she could attract men this way and still keep them at bay before any real damage was done.

Her smile was a killer and whenever she would switch off and rebuff any further action, the men usually accepted her decision without too much of a protest or any indication of violence. She just said 'no' so nicely. They shrugged, thanked her for her company and moved on to another, more inebriated girl who would grant them more liberties. Aida would sometimes disappear for short periods with one conquest or another and Milduta knew she did 'it'. She admired her friend's courage and lack of scruples but she knew that she wanted her own first total sex experience to be different. She didn't wish to be yet another young Estonian teen fuck against the wall of a decrepit building or in the back room of a municipal bar.

Maybe she was an idealist, but she still thought there should be something different about it. Some dignity at least. The notion of love was alien to her, thanks to her parents' sad influence, and her cold heart had always remained of ice when watching the soppy romantic stories, mostly French movies, so popular at the local cinema. She much preferred the comedies with Bourvil or Fernandel. They were absolutely hilarious.

But the call of lust was strong as well as bewildering.

So, Milduta allowed the men who bought her drinks to caress her body with their roving hands as she slid across the busy dance floor, clumsily fingering her through her skirt. She allowed them the public foreplay, this overture to fucking. But she knew she was not yet ready to give herself, to be fucked.

Not that the thought didn't keep her awake at night. Much too often.

One man, a local businessman who was a regular at the bar she and Aida attended most Saturday evenings, had loaned her book. A translation of the French novel 'The Story of O'.

Milduta had found it compelling.

Only the story could make her wet, not the rough and amateur hands of men. She masturbated to it on a regular basis.

Imagined herself as a similar slave.

Used beyond the bounds of the imagination. Whipped. Tortured. Obscenely displayed to crowds. Her openings stretched. Ringed.

The idea of the ring just took her breath away and she always came so strong when she read or simply remembered that part of the heroine's ordeal.

Or maybe it was the exquisite elegance of the setting, the castle with all its finery, the sophistication of the men and other women in residence at Roissy. It was such a marked contrast to the smoke-filled, low-ceilinged buildings of Tallinn and its ever-grey sky. Estonia's ever-present smell of chemical disinfectant and drunks being sick with metronomic regularity all over the town as Saturday night moved on. Surely, sexual pleasure belonged to a better climate.

Between sixteen and eighteen, her final years at college, Milduta continued to resist the Rubicon of sex, while all the time its attraction grew stronger in her mind than her body's actual demands. For that, she had her fingers. As if she already knew that when the time came, normal sex might actually not prove enough for her confused needs. In the meantime, all those mad thoughts of the horrors and delights of sex flew across her dreams and nights, confirmation to her that all the callow boys she had gone out with were not for her. The darker side of older men tempted her greatly.

Maybe, she reckoned, when she went to Business and Administration school – a step she had readily agreed to when her grandparents had suggested she should continue her education – things would change and sex would begin to mean something.

There might be other types of men than those she had so far come across in her restricted journeys on the East side of Tallinn.

Milduta firmly hoped so.

9

Of course, Jack had dreams.

Some were quite absurd; rambling and disjointed tissues of illogical non sequiturs and randomly spaced events that any psychiatrist would enjoy a field day with. Others were just plain confused. And then some made sad sense.

In all of them, Pierre was impeccably dressed: the cut of his suits exemplary and no crease more than a half-inch out of position; the cloth elegant and fashionable, Prince de Galles patterns or darker shades of brown. His pullovers were always made out of cashmere, usually in muted red or variations of orange. Shirts, either white or pale blue and meticulously pressed (unlike Jack's shirts which were always of the drip-dry variety). His shoes carefully polished to a shine. Outerwear from Burberry. The veritable image the French provinces would have of an Englishman of leisure. If he had the necessary cash, that is. And a decade or so out of date.

Pierre stood, dark-eyed, in Jack's dreams.

And then with a nonsensical cut jump, there he was fucking Catherine as Jack sat in the cheap seats, cowering, hypnotised by the shocking spectacle.

Jack had, of course, seen photographs of the naked human body and sometimes closer glimpses of other boys in the dressing room at the football ground, or when they were changing at the swimming pool, but had never seen either Pierre – much less Catherine – in the altogether, so his imagination supplied the scene with painful features abundant.

Her slight, pale frame in ecstatic repose; her nipples an

exaggerated shade of red, like a Renaissance madonna in a museum or art book painting, jutting upwards as she was stretched out over a pale sheet on the bed; her legs held unseemly apart by the weight of the young man thrusting in and out of her.

Passive and mute, like a sacrificial virgin offered to the gods. Which reminded Jack that, during the course of that fateful conversation, he had not asked her whether it had been her first time or not.

On every occasion he played that momentous scene back to himself on the sordid screen that lurked at the back of his mind, Jack always conceived of it as a silent movie, even though his masochist heart begged for sound. To hear how she moaned, cried out, sighed as Pierre plugged her remorselessly, from pleasure or pain, or the sweet and no doubt obscene words Pierre whispered in her ear as he systematically plundered her insides with his vile cock.

But the imaginary movie insisted on remaining silent. Not that he would have needed subtitles to translate their pillow French.

Their fucking – he couldn't bring himself to think of it as lovemaking – brought bitter tears to his eyes.

And, shamefully, invariably caused his involuntary erection as the camera he couldn't control zoomed in on the fornicating couple at regular intervals to catch every single detail of their actions in full anatomical close-up.

A hostage to his dreams, Jack sat immobilised in his seat, his cock rock-hard and painful, straining to move his eyes even closer still to their heaving, sweating bodies. Observing the movement of Pierre's thick penis breaching her entrance time and time again, its veiny trunk brushing past the tight lips, stretching her open with renewed vigour with every pumping movement forward. A meticulous director, Jack began adding details to the scene. He imagined from her thin hair that her pubes must be sparse. That Pierre's cock was uncut and that his foreskin would hang loose around his glans as he inserted himself into her forcibly, cramming every inch of meat and flesh inside her body (Jack's knowledge of genital anatomy was still unformed and prone to minor mistakes in those early years; had he had knowledge of the real mechanics of sex – the humidity, the smells, the secretions, the awkwardness – he would no doubt have converted his inner movie to 3D or Sensurround and rivalled producer and director William Castle with the gaudy realism of his special effects in a bid to bring the haunting event to life).

All in his fevered imagination, however, as he struggled to distinguish even more garish details of the fuck in progress, every single movement was like a dagger aimed at his own stomach, a consummate form of self-torture.

For the stark grossness of hardcore action, Jack would, however, have to wait some more years until his first trip to Scandinavia where such films were legal and he would, following business appointments during the day, haunt the backstreets of Copenhagen and Stockholm in his lonely evenings to witness the copulation of others at first hand and on a real screen.

He quickly found this spectacle both repetitive and surprisingly lacking in artistry and tenderness, as well as in the necessary aggression he'd half expected from his own warped imagination.

The pornography of others was no match for his.

Even though, to the best of his limited knowledge, neither Pierre nor Catherine later pursued a professional career in sex movies. She wasn't opulent enough, anyway, he reflected much later. A mere teenage French girl who had briefly captured his heartstrings and unwittingly wounded him, bringing his romantic dreams down to earth with a hell of a jolt.

Three or four women later, he'd even reflect in amazement on what in her could even have attracted him.

How flimsy the rules of attraction can be, he'd smile.

But right then, in the full bloom of teenage angst, the pain was worse than excruciating.

10

Jack had never thought of himself as a violent person. He'd always carefully avoided conflict; at school, even when direly provoked on occasion, or in his relationship with his parents, despite a tetchy rapport with his father.

But the scar that damn Pierre had left imprinted on his mind, and the way he'd dirtied Catherine forever, screamed for revenge.

Inspired by his first term of philosophy studies, Jack, who'd always a gift for telling stories, had decided to write a novel. This magnum opus was to be full of symbolism and metaphors and deal with reincarnation, a fictional theme he couldn't get out of his mind since reading H Rider Haggard's *She* and falling under the compelling spell of Ayesha. The ghost of Catherine paled against the shadow of the immortal African queen. Somewhere in the story he'd devised was to feature a long list of famous writers who had also committed suicide, and Jack had thoroughly researched the subject on the bookshelves of the French Institute where he often spent his lunch breaks.

He had laid out a chart listing all the methods of death available to the would-be suicide. From bullet and dagger to poison to rope and gas and beyond, the ensuing results were anything but a cheerful panorama of manic depression taken a step too far.

Shortly before the Easter-term break, confronted once too often by Pierre's ever-present smug and contented smile, Jack realised to his dismay that he harboured thoughts of murder.

Surely Pierre must pay.

In his mind, he reasoned Pierre had taken what was his.

And the jealousy was eating him up inside.

However, at seventeen, you have neither the imagination nor the means.

Jack reviewed his master suicide list from the now stalled novel, and considered methods he might conceivably get away with. Noting the minutiae of brutal demise and execution, he carefully jotted down pointers in pages from an old diary, gleaning the necessary technical information from the crime and mystery paperbacks he had read with voracious appetite in his earlier teens: a panoply of pulp authors like James Hadley Chase, Brett Halliday, Peter Cheyney, Claude Rank, Jean Bruce. They weren't that informative when it came to the daily reality of crime, even if the latter French writer had a knack for sophisticated and provocative devices of sexual torture when his spy hero or his female acolytes got captured, usually once per book, by the Eastern European or yellow villains. Which often provided Jack with unavoidable erections. But he soon came to the conclusion that he was far from prepared to commit murder, let alone not arouse suspicion in the process. It all looked so much easier on paper.

His best chance was for Pierre to be run over by a bus, but Jack knew he hadn't the courage or the guile to be the one to shadow him for hours on end and then push him firmly under the killing wheels when no one else was looking.

So Pierre survived.

But Jack, disgusted at his own lack of moral fibre and annoyed by the streak of cowardice he had discovered in his veins, swore blindly that he would never accept betrayal of the heart so meekly again. If there was to be another time, even years down the road, he would be firmer, more decisive and would take the matter into his own hands.

He would meet other women.

Many would end up wounding him in different ways. But the betrayal or sense of loss never hurt him so deep again.

He would learn to live with occasional rejection, or the subtle erosion of a love affair, but it never involved sexual jealousy.

Until Milduta.

11

When she turned eighteen Milduta rid herself of her shoulder-length hair. A symbolic rite of passage on her calculated road to adulthood.

The local hairdresser, under precise instructions, trimmed her flowing auburn locks to mid neck. Not too boyish, she felt, but no longer as girlish as it had previously been. Her grand-parents howled in protest. How could she ruin her looks so thoughtlessly? Milduta argued the cut was so much more modern, but their generation still cherished hair falling down a woman's back, and the attendant care and endless brushing to keep it supple and silky.

She began her classes at the Business school on the other side of Tallinn.

Yeltsin had just taken over from Gorbachev over the border in Russia, following the failed communist putsch, and Glasnost was in its heyday.

Milduta had had to join the young pioneers five years earlier, at her grandparents' instigation. This has enabled her to go on cheap group holidays with other kids of her age, which she had enjoyed. It was on one of these trips to the sandy. Nidas beaches of Lithuania that she had first met Aida, who had become her best friend. They had graduated together to the ranks of the Komsomol where they'd even trained together in military classes and learned how to strip down a gun with their eyes closed. Milduta had actually been the best performer in her age group. Aida dropped out of college during their last year and took a job as a receptionist for one of the big hotels.

To coincide with the official end of communism, Milduta had ceremonially torn up her membership card, along with most of her new classmates, at the end of their first week of courses. There had been copious amounts of drinking and someone had suggested they do this as their concession to the new, emerging market economy, to signify the new direction in their business studies. Most of the serious young men also studying there dreamed of capitalism and its gifts, but Milduta held no illusion about her own personal goals. She was sublimely indifferent to the market, the complexity of currency transactions and the restructuring of the old, centralised economy into an entrepreneurial cluster of thriving private businesses. Money was there to be spent and she seldom worried about what tomorrow would bring. She was confident she would manage. Now technically an adult, she just wished to enjoy her life; face problems when they occurred and not worry about them before the fact. She only attended the school because her now rapidly ageing grandfather believed she would meet a better kind of man there.

This was not the case, as she soon discovered. All in all, the earnest young men who attended the Business school were more refined than the men and boys she would meet in the clubs and bars in her own part of town, but most had little time or interest in the fairer sex. Money and wealth was their god and everything else was a distraction. There were, of course, exceptions but, paradoxically, they were also the more mediocre students.

At least they enjoyed Milduta's company on the rare social occasions some of them would get together for a birthday, or to celebrate an exam or the halting progress of the local soccer club in the UEFA Cup. She was chirpy and cheerful and had such a wonderful smile and didn't mind roving hands, within reason. So her presence was tolerated even if she didn't truly fit into their rarefied group.

She felt they treated her condescendingly, as if she were one of their younger sisters.

And no way was it the way she thought of herself.

She was a woman, damn it.

So, she fled their company outside school hours and days and joined Aida again on her drinking and dancing forays into the clubs on the West side of town.

They had their routine down pat and frequently managed whole evenings, or even all-nighters, without having to pay for a single drink. It was fun.

Men were fools.

Milduta now believed that the men who courted her would stay content if she sometimes allowed herself to be kissed. Real kisses, of course, with tongues. It pleased them briefly, but quite failed to satisfy her. What was so pleasurable about this awkward intimacy, after all? Too many of them tasted of stale alcohol and tobacco and she found the experience of kissing her dance partners, and erstwhile would-be boyfriends, most definitely unpleasant.

And as the evenings lengthened she knew their hands, encouraged by their locked lips, would venture further around and across her body, maybe slip under her corsage or skirt, until their frustration at her passive demeanour would come to the boil and they would suggest sex; or downright demand it.

She confided in Aida.

'They are beginning to think I am just a tease,' she said. 'But none of them attract me enough to do the deed. I know it's silly: I take advantage of them but I can't not hold back. It's just that I want the first one to be special.'

'It doesn't hurt that much, you know, Mimi,' Aida tried to reassure her. Just a fortnight earlier, she had had her first abortion.

'So you say,' Milduta answered. 'But that's not the point. Really...'

They were sitting on elevated bar stools, disco rhythms punctuating the din in the dance club, nursing double measures of Polish vodka laced with apricot juice. A gargantuan sailor moved towards them and suggested a dance.

They both declined.

'You have to give them the feeling they've gained something from you,' Aida tried to explain.

'They paw me, stroke my butt, knead my tits... What else can I allow them?' Milduta queried. 'Just last week, Milan even tried to push his finger into my arse crack while we were dancing. A good thing I was wearing that old woollen skirt. He was rubbing himself against me on and on. He was so hard I thought it was about to burst through his jeans.'

'You should give them some relief,' Aida suggested. 'They're only men, they're only human. They have needs too.'

'How?'

'They don't mind if you help them with your hand. But they love it if a girl uses her mouth, you know.'

Milduta blanched in the penumbra of the noisy club. She had heard of the practice. The idea alone gave her goose bumps.

She agreed to consider it.

Aida called it a blow job.

She even agreed to demonstrate for her friend.

'A Coca-Cola bottle or a banana will do,' she grinned.

12

By the time Jack had moved back to Paris, Catherine was already part and parcel of the past and the new world was full of blondes.

Elizabeth was the first to break his heart.

Well, you have to begin somewhere.

And prior to the pain there were at least months of joy.

As a student he had lived a life of squalor, sharing a small apartment near the Halles with another guy, though neither of them cleaned the place with much alacrity or regularity. Fortunately, Alphonse and he had quite different taste in women, which made their cohabitation comfortable.

He had just broken up with a French medical student called Danielle a few days before his birthday party. They'd just grown tired of each other and the sex had never really been that good anyway, but it was the timing of the parting that annoyed Jack most. He was sorry not to have a girlfriend at birthday time.

Traditionally, Jack and Alphonse, whose own birthday fell just two weeks earlier, threw a massive open-door party for the occasion, inviting everyone they both knew and allowing friends to bring whoever they felt like. It was a way of repaying favours all around and ensuring they would themselves keep being invited to others' parties. The booze always flowed in liberal quantities, as all guests were required to bring along a few bottles at least. The consequent mess and filth in the apartment in the aftermath of these parties were so comprehensive that they actually had to scrub and clean the place most thoroughly to bring it back to a decent level of hygiene. As good an excuse as any other to have the party, the two young men reckoned.

Half the people who had turned up Jack didn't even know. Friends of friends or even, he assumed, total strangers who'd heard a party was on from a conversation in a bar or the University corridors. Much of the crowd even spilled out on to the landing, as both rooms of the apartment were already full. Jack navigated, glass in hand, between the mass of guests, drowning his womanless sorrow with marked lack of joviality.

At some stage, another Brit introduced himself and handed Jack his card, thanking him for the generous invitation. Jack, over the din of the music and the dozens of criss-crossing conversations and laughter, didn't even catch who the guy had crashed the party with. At any rate, he was inviting him to another party the following day, somewhere in the 16th arrondissement.

Shortly after this brief conversation, someone handed Jack a label-less bottle which he proceeded to incautiously gulp down and he quickly passed out, blissfully missing the last hours of his own birthday celebration.

He awoke to the repugnant smell of rancid booze, cigarette ash and stagnant air midway through the next morning and was promptly sick, adding vomit to the palette of dubious smells that now permeated the apartment through and through. Alphonse had escaped the landscape after the battle and gone to sleep things off at his current girlfriend's nearby flat.

A walk down the boulevard to the Left Bank cleared his mind and thinned his hangover, by which time the sky was already darkening, and Jack felt no compulsion to stay in amongst the dregs of the party. They'd clean up Monday without fail, when Alphonse was back.

He changed into a clean shirt and a newer pair of jeans and looked up the address of the party on the map. It was a part of Paris he seldom visited, too bourgeois for his taste. Too expensive, too.

He recognised many of the faces in the crowd from previous get-togethers. The usual expatriate crowd, mostly. Brits on secondment to overseas branches of banks, insurance companies or the local multinationals. A somewhat boring group of folk, he felt. And his own lack of cheerfulness certainly contributed little to warming the atmosphere, as he moved from buffet to wall and back to buffet again and again in a bid not to sprout roots.

He had decided to return home when the doorbell rang and the host opened the front door of the upmarket flat to let in two young women he had not previously come across in Paris. His eyes were immediately taken by the brunette. Lustrous dark curls and a remarkable pallor. And lips to kill for. The two newcomers threw their coats onto one of the beds in the adjacent room and walked up to the table where the bottles and plastic cups were laid out. Jack couldn't keep his eyes off the shorter of the two young women. Her companion was blonde, slim and looked very English but she didn't impinge unduly on his consciousness at this stage.

A few couples were distractedly dancing to some tunes filtering through from the hi-fi, tended to by the wife of the Assistant Manager of the Paris branch of Lloyds. Mostly rock or Motown tunes.

The two women were in deep conversation with some OECD executives in the other corner of the main room.

Jack, on the spur of the moment, decided he would invite the pretty, dark-haired woman to dance. Not that he was a good dancer, or even enjoyed dancing. But it was a way of starting a conversation, he supposed. Meeting her. But the music had to be right. And slower.

He lurked and waited for the right opportunity.

When it came – a syrupy Peggy Lee song – he took a few steps towards the two women, now talking to each other and that bore Roland Thompson. Just a few strides across the room. But as he almost reached them, the brunette and bloody Thompson nodded at each other and inched back to take position in the exiguous dance area not occupied by drinkers.

Jack found himself facing the friend, the blonde.

She looked up at him.

She had grey eyes.

'Hello,' she said.

He couldn't walk away, could he?

'I was wondering whether you might like to dance?' he suggested, to cover up his embarrassment.

'I'd love to,' she replied.

She put her arm forward so he could lead.

'I'm Elizabeth,' she said.

'Jack.'

One hour later, they left the party together.

For two hours they walked, crossing half of Paris, following the river. He would never recall if it had been a cold night or not.

She was staying in a small hotel near the Place de la Republique, with her girlfriend. They had only arrived in Paris a week earlier, to take up secretarial positions at the British Chamber of Commerce, and were still looking for accommodation.

They never reached the hotel and three hours after meeting Elizabeth, she was in his bed.

13

Until now, Milduta had never given undue consideration to the subject of men's cocks.

They existed, they were there, a bit like objects, dark and dangerous that lurked inside men's pants; instruments of pleasure if she slavishly believed what she read in books, poles of procreation according to the school and family doctors who had so far treated and advised her, as well as the rare bits of advice her grandparents had reluctantly doled out.

She had several times seen her brother's, when they were smaller, but it had left no lasting memory. Just an extraneous and slightly ridiculous growth that just dangled there, uselessly. All she remembered thinking at the time was that a penis must be a bit of a nuisance when it came to dressing, having to find its rightful position in one's underwear and all that. She much preferred her own female opening: more discrete and practical to pee surely.

Her first thought when Aida had suggested she become better acquainted on a personal basis with men's genitalia, was whether she would manage to refrain from bursting into giggles when a man presented his pride and glory for her to lick or suck. The whole idea appeared so absurd.

But her friend reminded her that there was no pain involved.

'It's easy, you see. Think of it as having to suck an ice lolly, although cocks are warmer and have barely any taste.'

'Really?'

'Well, hopefully, the guys are clean,' her friend had contorted her lips in a gesture of repugnance. 'Most are.'

'I see,' Milduta had acquiesced.

'And you stay a virgin until you think the time, and the guy, is right,' Aida added. 'And no worries about possible pregnancy either.'

'That's an important consideration,' Milduta remarked. She had no wish to have a baby this early. She'd witnessed too many girls in her part of town having children while still in their teens and noted how much it affected their lives.

'And the men are happy?' she queried her friend. 'They pressure you less afterwards to open your legs for them?'

'Oh, they love it,' Aida answered. 'Sure, they might still suggest you let them fuck you, but they're spent for some time. There's less pressure. You can always hint you'll go further once you've been with them more often. They're gullible. You suck their cock and they stop thinking straight.'

'So why do you open your legs to them, Aida?' Milduta asked.

'I like it, Milduta. It's a nice feeling inside. Or maybe I'm just a slut. I'm not like you: I don't go to Business school. I haven't the choice of men. One day I'll choose one who's just about OK, who's affectionate, doesn't drink to excess, maybe, and I'll settle down. But not quite yet. In the meantime, I just want to enjoy life, Milduta.'

Milduta sighed. Despite her worldly ways, she knew her friend was also naive and she feared for her.

'The abortion the other month, what happened?' she questioned Aida. She knew her girlfriend had been in pain and ever so sad for days afterwards.

Fortunately, the boy responsible had been a student from the nearby Polytechnic, and when Aida had informed him of the pregnancy, he had downright panicked and managed to convince his middle-order, Town Hall functionary parents to supply the cash for the termination while there was still time. They had even selected the doctor themselves to ensure there was no fuck-up which would have badly reflected on them and their son. Since then, the young man had transferred to Vilnius in Lithuania to continue his studies.

'The bloody condom leaked, I think. It was an accident. The local ones are such poor quality. But the imported ones from Sweden are too expensive. Anyway, when I go with men now, I don't open my legs any more.'

'You just give them…' Milduta still had a problem referring to blow jobs.

'No,' Aida lowered her eyes, 'sometimes, not always, I let them use my other… hole.'

Milduta blushed deep red and fell silent.

'It's somewhere they can put it in,' Aida tried to justify herself, 'and there's no damn risk of falling pregnant.'

'Doesn't it hurt?' Milduta asked, still grappling with the whole concept of a man inserting his penis into a woman's anus, something she had never heard of before or even dreamed of in her wildest imagination. Maybe the act had been alluded to in 'The Story of O' but if it had, she had probably misunderstood it.

'It can, a little,' her friend had replied. 'Specially, if the guy's thing is large. But I'm used to it now… and it's safe.' She looked towards Milduta. It was a Saturday morning and they were sitting in a milk bar. 'Do you think badly of me?'

'No,' Milduta answered. 'Your life amazes me. I never thought… When the men enter you there, does it give you any pleasure?'

'It doesn't.' Aida replied. ' But I ask them to touch my pussy while they fuck my rear. It helps a bit.'

'I think I'll confine myself to sucking them,' Milduta reflected, her mind still agog from these new revelations. But she was determined to retain her popularity and knew she had to put out more on their evenings out. If that was what men wanted from her, that's what she would give them for now. After all, it sounded harmless, if a bit yucky. It was just a penis, after all, and her mouth and tongue. She'd still be the same after. Wouldn't she?

She couldn't go out with her friend that weekend because it was her grandmother's birthday, but all week long she couldn't help thinking of men's cocks and what she was determined to graduate to the following weekend.

On one hand, part of her felt the whole exercise of taking a man's small, shrivelled penis into her mouth bordered on the ridiculous, but another part of her was deadly curious to discover what it would feel like to experience one actually swelling up and growing under her lips, as she knew it would. Or would her tongue have a stronger effect on it, she wondered. Aida had mentioned taste, but was it the flavour of the actual skin of the cock, or was she referring to the taste of the liquid that would emerge from it when the man ejaculated. Should she swallow it? Spit it out? Would the hard cock inside her mouth have a particular texture?

These thoughts took over her imagination and she was seriously unable to concentrate on her classes on company overheads (and how to keep them under control) and the setting up of letters of credit.

14

Elizabeth was much more sexually experienced than Jack and many years later, when his heart had settled down sufficiently from the initial hurt and confusion to reflect on the relationship, he would marvel at how in hell he had managed to hold on to her for all of six months.

Or how, that first evening, he could have even briefly considered Rose, her dark-haired friend.

Elizabeth came from Greenwich, in South London, and her hair was the colour of straw, cut straight with a short fringe dissecting her forehead, not unlike the style of Jean Shrimpton, the model of the moment. She and Rose had only recently completed a year together at a secretarial college in New Cross and had decided to try Paris for a year so; a different city, a different life. Neither spoke much French but they had a sense of adventure and dreamed of the overt romanticism of French men. Ironically, both ended up with British boyfriends within a month of their arrival in the French city.

The previous women Jack had walked out with or fucked in Paris had mostly been French and he had met most of them through University seminars, lectures and corridors. Some also studied Comparative Literature, while others were from the close-by Medical Faculty. The nice Jewish girls his family had thrown his way lacked spice or intellect. Alphonse's hunting patch was at the Beaux Arts, the riotous art school, closer to the Seine. They were altogether different sorts of creatures, wild and gypsy-like and dreadfully fascinating, but much to dangerous for the likes of Jack who, at heart, was very cautious and conservative.

Elizabeth was perfect for him.

She was easy-going, undemanding, ever-cheerful and impervious to mood swings, a shining blonde and, to him at least, looked like a fashion model racing across the streets of swinging London, not unlike Julie Christie in the film Bill Liar; an icon if ever there was one.

A week after meeting and bedding her, he still couldn't believe his luck. Women like her never fell for complicated, brooding men like him, did they? Somehow it didn't feel like part of the script.

She had small, pale breasts he loved to caress with the sheer tip of his fingers. Her pink nipples hardened under his fleeting contact and he would delicately draw a nail across them and watch her close her eyes and shudder. Jesus, she was beautiful; a living doll for his play and pleasure. She was also the first woman to hardily take his hard cock into her hands and stroke him to even more desire as they embraced. The previous girls in his life had had a strange relationship with his penis; tolerating its existence, accepting its penetration when they fornicated, but otherwise indifferent to its presence. Only a prostitute, one drunken evening shortly after his arrival in Paris to attend University, had actually ever taken him, it, into her mouth.

The way Elizabeth would tend to his cock felt so innocent and natural and lacked any kind of vulgarity. They would often lie together in post-coital contentment and she would allow her hand to linger over his side, creep slowly against his detumescent organ and would sometimes pick the pitiful piece of meat up between two extended fingers, as if to weigh it, and noting its lack of ardour would gently proceed to awaken it with measured movements and ministrations until he was ready to fuck her again, or feebly spurt another meagre ration of his seed into her palm. This, she always did in total silence, just the quiet sound of their breath punctuating the emptiness of the bedroom. She also came with nary a word, unlike the majority of the French girls before her who made it a point of expressing their pleasure with the loudest of moans, cries, sighs or, on one unforgettable occasion with Danielle, a moment-by-moment football-like commentary on the ever-growing rise of her orgasm, culminating with a chosen string of anti-religious obscenities and even a loud fart as her whole body lost control and gave in to the waves of inner ecstasy flooding her from every angle of her emotions.

It worried Jack that Elizabeth so seldom made a sound when she came.

'Did you come?'

'Yes...'

'You were so quiet...'

'I'm just reserved, Jack. It was good. Don't you worry.'

Her pubic hair was short and intensely curly, thus initiating another of his lifelong obsessions with women's cunts and their vegetation, as he found he could gaze at her naked crotch for ages and never tire of its sight.

'You're a dirty young man, Jack. You shouldn't look at my pussy that much, it's not right. Makes me feel self-conscious. Dirty.'

'Not at all. It's just beautiful, you know. Really.'

'Hmmm.'

It was also a shade or two darker than her mid shoulder-length, straight, blonde hair. This puzzled him mightily, but he put this down as a minor anomaly, ignorant as he was then of hydrogen peroxide and its cosmetic uses.

For months, they fucked like rabbits.

Elizabeth never initiated the sex, but neither did she ever mind.

When she had her period, she would grant him hand jobs to relieve his frustration.

Jack felt he would never tire of her.

Not that they spoke much between fucks. They walked light-hearted along the Paris streets; window-shopped;

caught movies; attended parties where all the guys envied
him because of her short skirts and great legs; she gossiped
about her work; he improvised his plans for world domination of science fiction writing; and then it was time to have
sex again, in a friend's spare bedroom at whatever party, on a
street corner, standing, under cover of darkness when the
nearest bed was still too far, or back at Jack's apartment, if
Alphonse and his confusing array of girlfriends were not
already using the bedroom.

They fucked like rabbits.

He knew Elizabeth found him fun, and ever so slightly different from the other men she had known prior to meeting
him. This suited him perfectly. However, Jack soon committed
the capital error of mistaking her uncomplicated willingness
and sexual availability for what it wasn't. He fell in love with
her.

One day while she was sleeping, he stole away into the
other room and began reading pages from her diary, which he
had earlier spotted peering out from her abandoned handbag
on the kitchen table.

Here, he discovered that on their first encounter she had
found him darkly foreign, whatever that meant.

He also found out that she had left behind a veritable
stream of lovers in London. Every sexual encounter there
merited a lengthy description and assessment, and new and
extreme sexual variations he could barely imagine, let alone
had even experienced in Elizabeth's arms. He raced through
the pages and, to his bitter disappointment, found he didn't
rate very high indeed in her sexual pantheon. Willing but lacks
imagination was her conclusion.

So he was far from surprised when, a few weeks later,
Elizabeth finally tired of him.

She broke the news gently.

No, there was no one else, but she just felt their affair had
come to the end of its term. She was not seeking anything permanent and she feared he was getting too serious about the

whole thing. Fun while it lasted, no? And she was not ready for commitment or anything permanent.

Jack took it badly.

15

So, while too many of her childhood friends were losing their virginity time and time again on the cheap – after all, best to convince every new guy he was the first so he might not be too rough – whether in the back of patched-up cars or in the semi-darkness of badly lit backyards of local jazz or drinking clubs, or, when all other locations lacked the necessary privacy, the damp fields that bordered the funfair permanently installed in the grounds that separated the municipal park from the chemical factory, Milduta, by default, became the blow-job queen of West Tallinn.

After all, she reflected, it's harmless.

And it wasn't even as if she had sucked any man's cock that readily. Usually, she would manage to string them along for a couple of weeks at least, enjoying drinks, maybe a restaurant meal and a movie, before she reckoned she had to return the favour in kind. Testing the ground thus helped her sort out the good ones from the bad ones. It was easy to predict which were too heavy drinkers or likely to use violence after a few dances or evenings. Actually, she preferred them a little shy. They had more respect for her as a woman. And proved easier to manipulate, at least until pay day.

The first guy she took to the empty cloakroom at a Saturday night ball groaned with pleasure as she licked him slowly and shyly took him whole, shook briefly within seconds in his whole body, and sharply pulled his cock out of her mouth and spurted onto the nearby wall. It only took a minute or so and it was all over. He hadn't even grown fully hard. She'd never known men could ejaculate while still partly soft.

Milduta was even a bit disappointed. She hadn't had the chance to assess his taste, his texture or got a real hold on his cock. Just a rapid in and out. Almost too easy.

He'd even profusely apologised to her after he'd pulled his trousers up.

The following week, at another dance, he'd deliberately avoided her. Maybe he was ashamed that he couldn't hold on long enough, she guessed.

At the end of the spring term, she only managed a middle grade at her exams and decided she wasn't truly cut out for a career in commerce. She found a job as a purchase ledger book-keeper in the offices of the local chocolate factory. The other women there were zombies; middle-aged women with no sense of fun who could only talk of their kids or the weather, or complain endlessly about their husbands during the coffee breaks.

She wasn't earning a fortune but at least it provided her with some measure of independence.

Initially, she reasoned that with enough money in her wallet, she would no longer need to play along with men in the evening for the drinks and small favours they bestowed against a pleasant smile or later the service of her mouth, but she found she actually enjoyed toying with them. And sucking their cocks. She couldn't even say that she overly enjoyed the company of men. The better dancers among them already had regular girlfriends for the most. And what else were guys of use to her for?

But the truth is that she now enjoyed the game of take and give that she played with men. She felt good about using them, and somehow didn't feel she was being used. It was a trade. In the new market economy that now dominated the crumbling Soviet bloc, trade was what made the world go round.

And she had that bizarre feeling of daring anticipation inside her, deep in the pit of her stomach, inside the increasing stickiness of her cunt, at the outset of every outing, every bar, each new adventure; wondering in advance which guy she would end up with tonight, the look that would light up his face when she said no to sex but suggested she blow him; the likely size of his organ, even the colour of his often frayed underwear or where they would actually do it.

She perfected her technique when they stayed hard long enough, took pride in her delicacy and know-how.

Some liked her to hold their cock while she sucked.

Others would rather she just impale her mouth and not touch them.

Then there were those who would slip their fingers through her hair and rub her scalp to accompany her oral activity, sometimes even directing her movements. A few even tried to pull her hair to provide added urgency to her attentions, but she hated that and always warned them to stop instantly or else. Most demurred, anxious she not finish them off.

The rougher men often seemed overly keen on ramming their cocks as deep as they could manage, past the receptacle of her cheeks and almost down to her throat, and made her gag. But Milduta learned to conquer her instinctive reflex, would breathe deep and avoid retching and somehow managed to accommodate the cock and not interrupt its movement inside her warmth.

A few men even complimented her on her skill.

Milduta drew satisfaction from knowing she gave a good blow job.

And the fierce inner pride that assured her she was always the one in control

She did it because of the company men provided, the sheer force of the sexual desire they projected, even twice refusing money for it – once before the act by a musician she had taken a dislike to and refused to go with, and once after the act by a grateful middle-aged man, no doubt married, who had whispered sweet nothings in her ear as they danced together and convinced her she should gift him with her mouth as the evening drew to a close.

Milduta was angry he could have suggested she wanted money to suck him, and swore blithely at him for doing so, but was also secretly proud that he should have considered she was worthy of payment.

A year went by, slowly, punctuated by her boring work at the offices of the chocolate factory, the increasing weakness of her ageing grandparents and the routine of night life. Aida grew closer to a young man who was learning his trade locally as a car mechanic and moved out of town to follow him back to the countryside when his training came to an end.

By now, Milduta could barely remember how many cocks she had already sucked since that conversation with Aida at the milk bar, although she did absurdly recall she had ordered a raspberry shake that day. But she was still a virgin, even if one troublesome night the previous Christmas, one man had deemed the blow job insufficient and forcibly made her strip. She had, with tears in her voice, pleaded with him not to endanger her virginity and, faced by his erection coming to life again, had hesitantly suggested he plunder her other hole instead, remembering what Aida had said. He had tried but Milduta was too tight, even after he had roughly twisted two fingers into her to stretch her; fortunately, by then, all the alcohol he had consumed that night began to take its toll and he had grown small again and gave up the attempt in disgust.

Only fingers, she realised. Wasn't the same.

Milduta waited for the right man to come along.

And still wasn't too keen on swallowing their come, though...

16

Jack's suicide attempt had been far from earnest.

Much too melodramatic.

It was three weeks after the split from Elizabeth. He had called her at the typing pool where she awaited her permanent posting in the sprawling organisation and, pretexting something important, had asked her to come to his flat that evening at seven. She argued she already had something social set up, but Jack pleaded with her and insisted she cancel her assignation and see him. She reluctantly agreed. Adding that she hoped it was worth it.

The previous evening, a Sunday, he had spent all night outside her hotel, crouched and cold under an opposite doorway, waiting to see Rose and Elizabeth return from whatever party they had gone to. They never did, visibly spending the night somewhere else or, he sighed, with someone else. Once or twice he had closed his eyes from exhaustion, but the lights at their window had never come on. They must have gone to work directly from where they had stayed. The following morning he had taken his rash decision. Alphonse was out of town, visiting his parents in the South, so there was no risk of interruption.

A half hour before Elizabeth's arrival, Jack had slashed his wrists with a razor blade. Not having researched the realities of the subject, he didn't even realise that you should cut vertically along the arm, and not sideways across the wrist. It didn't really hurt, but the blood flowed impressively to begin with. He'd estimated he would still be safe and alive by the time Elizabeth arrived (he'd not locked the door).

He drowsed off as he heard her steps on the stairs.

'You fucking idiot!'

He sleepily opened his eyes and was surprised to see anger all over her features, and no sign of sorrow or sympathy. Let alone love.

She was very efficient, checked quickly on his wound, then called an ambulance.

Apart from earning him hefty bills later from the emergency services and the hospital, his pathetic call for attention (or was it pity?) failed to bring her back to him.

By the time, a week later – following a sharp ticking off from the doctors – that he returned to the apartment to pick up the pieces of his life again, Elizabeth had left instructions not to let his telephone calls through and was no longer living in the familiar cheap hotel near the Place de la Republique.

Within a month, she had decamped back to England.

And never responded to his frantic, apologetic letters.

A couple of years later, on a summer trip to London, he had managed to obtain her phone number in Greenwich and had called. By now his interest in her was mere curiosity, with much water having drifted under the bridges of his heart since. Her mother had answered. He pretended to be an old school friend of Elizabeth's who had lost contact with her. He learned she had married within six months of her return from Paris, which certainly surprised him. 'A lovely boy, a chartered accountant,' her mother had informed him with pride in her voice. Jack had quickly put the phone down and not responded further.

Even though his suicide attempt over Elizabeth had lacked gravitas, it set Jack on an increasingly obsessive path, focusing his thoughts on suicide and death. Years before Woody Allen similarly co-opted the subject, Jack already equated love and death in a strange, if logical, juxtaposition. He remembered the compulsive listings of dead writers he had compiled whilst back in London, during the philosophy classes. He expanded the field to not only authors who had committed suicide or been killed, but also actors, politicians, famous people. Carefully laid out columns for the varied methods of despatch: poison, knives, guns (broken down into manufacturers and calibre, of course), other accidents, whether suspicious or not...

He was not a cheerful young man, by any means, and his gloomy disposition wouldn't truly fade until he would hit thirty and had made love to a handful of blondes in an assortment of countries.

At least the research came to good use when he elected to do his Comparative Literature thesis on 'Aspects of Despair in Contemporary Literature', highlighting the doom-laden careers of F Scott Fitzgerald in America, Pierre Drieu la Rochelle in France and Cesare Pavese in Italy. Anything for a laugh!

Beretta.

Sig Sauer.

Colt.

Luger.

Smith & Wesson.

Sawn-off shotgun.

Digitalis.

Cyanide.

Rat poison.

Strangulation.

Smothering under a pillow.

Stabbing.

Cut throat.

Emasculation.

Electric shock.

Swiss Army knife.

Asphyxiation.

Carbon monoxide emissions.

Drowning.

He knew the list was far from exhaustive. But for now, it was a delightful and practical compendium of instruments of perfect murder and methods of revenge. Maybe some might come in handy one day, he reflected wryly.

17

Men's cocks had no particular taste, she discovered.

Their come did.

Initially, Milduta was surprised at the sheer diversity of cocks' shapes, sizes and appearance. They revealed themselves to her from the lurking darkness of trousers, briefs and jeans, each new one a minor revelation. Some were shrivelled to a point she even doubted her power to make them grow, or buried shyly within their own folds of slack, extraneous flesh; others emerged fully tumescent, magnificent instruments of virility, masts standing proud in the non-existent wind, at attention and eager for sweet and tender care.

There was little correlation between their eventual length and the man's own size or features. Or automatically between the colour of the cock itself or its attendant ball sac and the man's complexion. Some dark-haired guys had surprisingly pale, pink cocks, while fairer one displayed darker shades of brown or even purple.

Every cock she sucked was different, not that Milduta could remember too much about them following the act. They just became a memory, a particular smell. A distant scent of stale urine mostly, a remote whiff of shit on rare occasions, soap, deodorant, or just the natural odour of sweat, pungent, rancid, acrid, or just masculine.

They came mostly uncircumcised, sometimes cut, although the latter were few and far between since the local Jewish population had been decimated in WWII, when Estonia's attitude to Jews and her open collaboration with the occupying Nazi forces was a chapter many preferred to gloss over. There were few foreign students at Tallinn University; a crowd Milduta rarely mixed with. She had heard a wild rumour that many black men were not only cut but of massive proportion, but couldn't for the life of herself quite envisage the idea of entertaining a coloured man.

She also noticed that men whose foreskin had been removed at birth or later, for medical reasons, proved slightly less sensitive to the caress of her tongue, responding slower to her intimate contact, remaining hard longer and requiring more sustained work, even pain in her jaw, when their ultimate ejaculation was slow in coming.

But of course, it wasn't possible to know in advance what sort of cock she would be encountering with every new man she agreed to go with and please.

Like an adventure. Albeit one she was sometimes a little ashamed of. Her dirty secret, which none of her other friends knew about since Aida had moved away.

But the shame only lasted a few hours beyond an encounter, however messy it had been, and some were rather sordid, and as the deep longing inside her soul returned, she knew that come the evening, come a few drinks, she would consent again to being an instrument of pleasure and relief.

She knew by now that she had a reputation.

Sharply aware of the fact that men in the clubs and regular dances venues confided in each other, compared impressions of her oral skills, or drunkenly whispered to each other that the auburn-haired Milduta didn't mind sucking cock but never agreed to open her legs.

Some took this as a natural challenge to their personal abilities and powers of seduction and sweet talk, and it became gradually harder for her to deny them the ultimate satisfaction of a real fuck. By now, too many of the locals knew her ways, her familiar denials and protests and, on several occasions, she'd had to consent to being used anally as the satisfaction of her mouth failed to pacify their lust.

Every time, it hurt like hell, and Milduta felt soiled and damaged.

Also, the fact of standing, or more likely kneeling, naked next to a man felt awkward to her. Most blow jobs she ended up giving saw her keeping her clothes on, maybe just her top off. Being naked she was so much more vulnerable to their lust and probing eyes.

She knew she had a presentable body. Her breasts were small but nicely rounded and firm. Her navel elegantly turned inwards, her stomach was flat and her waistline high, highlighting her long, shapely legs. She considered her butt a little too square, but not large. She trimmed the hair around her pussy. And every man marvelled at the depth of her blue eyes. One even said he could literally drown in them. And they liked her smile. She was good company; one of them if they went out drinking, regardless of the sexual overtones or what they both knew would happen later. Others who mentioned her eyes were profoundly sad.

Mostly, Milduta knew how to please. Her mouth was adept at holding the cock in a gentle vice, squeezing it, savouring its girth, while her tongue worked on the glans inside with application and determination.

She was unconcerned by their adventurous hands roving across the parts of her body they could reach while she worked on their cocks. It kept them out of her knickers mostly and, her dark nipples proving particularly insensitive, she didn't overly mind their rough, often drunken hands grazing, twisting the tips of her boobs or kneading her slight breasts like soft clay.

They still appreciated her company, loved entertaining her, treating her to evenings out and often small presents; a scarf, a dress, foreign perfume.

A cock was a cock.

It wasn't even connected to the man. Just an instrument through which she rewarded them for their kindness.

It was, she reasoned, no more than a simple transaction. And did she ever try to justify it all to herself in moments of doubt: You want me to suck your cock?; Okay, I'll suck you but don't expect any more of me. It ain't for sale. My heart is not for the taking.

Because of her reputation, she seldom had regular boyfriends for long. Anyway, most she had persevered with ended up being quite boring. Just guys who loved her mouth and regularly came back for more of her services, even though they knew she was generous with her favours. Realists.

But she disliked men seeing all of her.

Nudity was a privilege she was unwilling to grant them willingly.

18

Unless the act took place under relative cover of darkness, Milduta would keep her eyes closed as she sucked the offered cocks of the men she went with.

In penumbra, there was a sense of anonymity, of being a nameless performer on the stage of some bizarre play whose script had been predetermined by an unknown power. She was just playing her part in an episode of the great war between the sexes; a great game full of anger, longing and inner fury. Just a cameo, a part player who had no moments of bravura or ambitions to scale the heights of the hills of desire. Just little Milduta the brave, budding blow-job queen of Tallinn, Estonia. An uncomplicated soul who was just puzzled as to where her true place lay in all this inner tumult.

Once the transaction had been agreed – and if all went her way and they proved sufficiently undemanding, no tits out or playing with herself for their viewing pleasure – she would loosen their belt and lower the trousers or jeans they were wearing and extricate their cock from its cosy refuge. She would move to her knees, assess its cleanliness, then gingerly open her mouth and move her lips towards the quivering cock, briefly teasing its tip with her tongue before surrounding its fleshy pole with all the velvet softness of her mouth.

Then, most often, she closed her eyes.

The act became almost mechanical. Her mind switched off and she allowed her imagination to run rampant. It helped pass the time. She would pretend she was blind as her tongue moved tentatively over the cock's head, swiftly avoiding any droplet of precum, licking its ridge with hungry curiosity, picturing the changing shades of pink, brown and purple of the aroused mushroom as it grew and vibrated inside her cheeks. She learned from men's reactions how to tease their openings – the small slit through which they also peed – with the pointed tip of her foraging tongue, noting the tremor of lust surging through the man's body as she did so, always careful to retreat in time before the man ejaculated so that the flow of his come would either just bathe her tongue or, preferably, fall outside her retreating mouth. If she was fully impaled on them, it was difficult to avoid her throat bearing the assault of the man's emissions.

Some men insisted she do it with lights on or in a well-lit place. She then hurried the service, her eyes bobbing up and down towards their pubes, her horizon limited by the matted forest of their heaving crotch. If she actually liked the guy, she would vary her movements and even shyly allow her tongue to roam across his dangling balls. One man ordered her to take his ball sac into her mouth. It felt curious but not unpleasant and gave her an even stronger feel of power over him. There was a foreign businessman she'd met at a hotel bar where she'd gone to celebrate an office colleague's birthday straight after work. He had suggested she come to his room. She pointed out she was not in it for the money and, with a smile, he'd agreed to her terms. Fellatio only. Once there, as she loosened his trousers, he begged to go naked. Milduta had briefly hesitated, but he seemed different from the others, an odd blend of ruthlessness and tenderness, so she agreed.

'You have a lovely body, my dear,' he'd remarked. She was grateful she was wearing her thong that day, unlike most weekdays when she sported unfashionable, if warm and practical, grey knickers. She'd purchased two black thongs on a recent weekend ferry trip to Gothenburg, in Sweden. She found them so daring.

He lay back on the bed, pulling his legs back over the quilt.

She had expected him to sit on the edge, with her facing him, on her knees, her head in the embrace of his thighs.

'So?' he inquired.

She moved towards the king-size bed and climbed on. Here she shuffled until she found the ideal position, the most convenient geometry to face his thick penis. Milduta ended up squatting slightly, bent over his cock, her weight shifting onto her heels. She took the foreigner into her mouth and within seconds became conscious that her posture stretched her cunt wide open. She felt sticky as her lower lips slowly parted. He smelled unusual, a whiff of foreign, expensive soap she was unfamiliar with.

She concentrated on the job at hand as the bed shifted slightly beneath their combined weight, its caster wheels unsteady across the hotel room floor.

She felt his hand caressing her arse. He was gentle.

His fingers moved down and soon entered her wetness.

She wanted to protest but with his other hand, the businessman held her head firmly down against his hard cock.

As he worked her cunt, his nails grazing against the acutely engorged clitoris, squeezing it, she felt the veins in his cock thudding against her mouth and, for the first time in ages, allowed the tide of pleasure to rise inside her.

As he poured into her mouth, she came with a ferocious surge of lust, concentric waves flooding out from the hub of her being, her fingered cunt. All of a sudden, she felt drained, a joyful exhaustion that prevented her from rising from the bed to spit out his ejaculate in the nearby sink. She was too tired to move and swallowed his expansive juice. She sighed.

The man purred. Equally spent.

'Are all Estonian virgins such good cocksuckers?' he asked her later, as she dressed.

'Just me,' she had answered.

If, right then, the foreign businessman had asked her for a fuck, she knew she would have agreed, ready to shed her hymen's blood on the sheets of the Forum Hotel.

She realised later that her resolve was beginning to falter. But would she ever find the right man here in Tallinn?

19

Nicky was the next woman to intersect his path. It was half a year after Elizabeth had flown to London.

Nicky was the youngest sister of one of his best friends in Paris and they somehow drifted together. Robert had a gaggle of brothers and sisters, ten of them, and sometimes Jack would notice someone in the street and almost guess they were related to Robert. They all had such distinctive, high cheekbones and square jaws. He would then invariably be introduced to them a few days later at a family gathering or party.

Robert was a cartoonist and Jack and he were playing around with an adult comic-strip project they wished to collaborate on, all the rage in France that year. Nothing ever came of it, though, once they'd devised the few spreads.

Nicky had light brown hair, cut short to the nape of her neck and, in a woman those cheekbones were to kill for, providing her features with a fascinating Oriental hint. You could see the family's wild antecedents from the Urals some centuries before and the mixed blood from the waves of invaders, from Genghis Khan to the Mongols. She was short and compact, with a tight, square arse he could almost hold in his outstretched hands.

He had known her for almost a year already. She was around, shadowing her brother at a gallery launch or publishing party, almost invisible, pleasant, ever-present, and Jack had sort of used gotten used to her presence.

On that occasion, Robert hadn't turned up and as the party ended, they had left the museum together and agreed to have a quick coffee before they went their own way.

They were about to cross the boulevard near the Bourse and it dawned on Jack that he had never really been alone with Nicky before. In fact, he had seldom spoken to her without a member of her family around. Until now, she had just been the younger sister who happened to be there. And had now grown past the age of eighteen.

And he noticed her scent. A strong, aggressive note that evoked a field of newly mown grass.

She stepped into the road, absorbed in their conversation. Jack looked up and saw a motorcycle rushing towards them. He quickly caught her hand and held her firmly back.

'Thanks,' Nicky said. 'It was silly of me, I just wasn't looking out.'

The traffic thinned out and they crossed together. She didn't pull her hand away from his.

He could feel her warmth move all the way through to his wrist.

They found a bar on the Rue Monsieur le Prince where they chatted for hours until it was time for her last metro home to the East of Paris where Robert's family lived.

'I'd like to see you again,' Robert hesitantly asked, gazing into her grey-green eyes.

'That would be nice,' Nicky replied.

'Just the two of us,' he added. 'No Robert or the others.'

She smiled.

'It was so great to be able to talk. I didn't know you before, if you see what I mean,' Nicky said.

'I know,' Jack agreed. 'I have exactly the same feeling.'

He kissed her cheek before she rushed down the metro steps.

They kept their friendship secret from family and friends. It would have been too complicated to explain, even if initially it was all quite innocent; holding hands, knees brushing together in movie houses, heartfelt conversations about art and politics until late at night.

Soon, Jack realised he was on that familiar and slippery

slope again. He was falling in love. Damn, was it a virus he had been infected with? He didn't wish to fall in love again. And then she was his best friend's sister, much too young for him, and would it not feel like taking advantage of her; her family who had accepted him in his midst with open arms; her brother? The omens were not good, he knew.

But she was the one to declare her love for him long before he had the courage to admit his own infatuation. There was generosity in her soul, her heart was open and available. And willing.

His own heart, or was it his brain, advised caution and much patience.

They messed about in bed, where he marvelled at the exquisite beauty of her body, but always drew back at actually having sex. He argued he respected her too much. She sulked, went all moody for days.

She left for her long pre-arranged Easter holidays in the South. In her absence, he searched his soul for agonising hours and realised that he was in love with Nicky too and there was no point procrastinating any further.

By the time she returned, Nicky's ardour for Jack had simmered down, quietened and, to his quiet despair, they drifted apart. The summer holidays came and she met another boy, nearer her age, and moved in with him shortly thereafter. Jack's only consolation was that she married the guy and was still with him twenty years later, as he was kept informed of her whereabouts and life through her brother.

Bad timing, Jack reckoned, and another lesson learned: never draw back from the love that is offered, because a love not taken will always find another place to settle.

With a heavy heart, he drew a final line in his mind under Nicky and concentrated on his burgeoning writing career. He began devising short crime stories in which the perfect crime always came undone because of a lack of attention to small details and deep-seated psychological flaws inherent to the main characters. He had even sold a couple of tales to small magazines, and had already graduated from the Department of First Stories. Beginner's luck!

20

Her grandfather died. A massive stroke. At least he didn't suffer.

Within three weeks, her grandmother was hospitalised and diagnosed with a terminal form of cancer affecting her liver. For months now she had borne the pain inside her gut in silence, afraid to complain for fear of worrying her husband and Milduta.

The doctor advised Milduta that it was only a question of weeks, at the most. There was nothing they could do and even the medicine to make the end less hard on her was in short supply and had to be kept for other patients with better prospects of survival. Milduta offered to take out a loan at the bank against her future wages, but was told it would just be waste of money. The hospital would ensure her grandmother didn't suffer too much, but they could not achieve the impossible.

The older woman she had always thought of as her real mother lingered on until the first rains of spring, and then faded quickly. She passed away in silence while Milduta was rearranging the assortment of flowers she had brought along in the cracked ceramic vase the hospital provided on the table next to every patient's bed. Just a moment before, Milduta had been telling her gran all the latest silly gossip from her office at the chocolate works. Her eyes had been wide open. And then she was no longer there.

Living alone in the apartment she had shared with her grandparents all her life proved unsettling; so full of memories and all the opportunities she had missed while they were both still alive to let them know how much she loved them. Her brother was now in the army and hadn't been able to attend either of the funerals.

She got promoted and now supervised the younger wages and pension clerks as well as the company's purchase ledgers, but she drifted through life like an automaton. She was hollow inside and felt so lost. By now, most of the girlfriends she'd known had moved on with their lives, settled down, even had kids. Even appeared reasonably happy, although they all complained about their husbands' drinking. But then it was the national vice and few were immune.

Milduta hadn't been to the Rhapsody Club for several years. She had heard on the local grapevine that it had been refurbished at some expense and was now patronised by a better class of guys.

'Little beauty, we haven't seen you here for ages. Welcome back.'

The barman on the early shift was still the same

'Let me see if I remember: you used to like gin and orange. A capitalist drink par excellence,' he sniggered.

She'd never been a great lover of vodka.

'Foreigners prefer their gin with tonic,' Milduta corrected him.

'A girl who likes to be different, no?'

She nodded indifferently.

Within a mere fifteen minutes of sitting on her own at the bar, she had her first approach.

'Refill?'

She barely looked up. The man had a faint Georgian accent. Maybe he'd lived or studied there.

'You offering?'

'Of course.'

'OK, I'll have the same.'

He ordered a Jack Daniels for himself. The choice of drink and his black silk suit betrayed his wealth.

'Thanks,' she said, as the barman swapped her empty glass for a full one.

'My pleasure,' the man said. 'What's your name?'

'Mimi,' she replied.

'Very nice. I'm Boris. Listen, I'm sitting at the table over there with some business friends,' he pointed at an alcove where four other men sat. 'Why don't you join us?' he asked. 'You must be all lonesome here.'

Milduta sighed. She was lonely, after all.

He offered his arm and guided her to the table.

Compared to local lads she knew, they held their drink better. Two of them were originally from Tallinn but they all worked in Georgia; something to do with import export. They were only back in town for two days, to finalise an important contract, and were now enjoying a quiet celebration.

They spoke of the delights of Tbilisi and the sturdy wooden dachas some of them owned on the Black Sea. One of the older Georgians assured her she was the spitting image of his daughter and that Estonian lasses had no right to be as pretty as his home-grown talent. The others flirted facetiously with her while the drinks generously flowed. Despite the sadness that still lurked inside her, Milduta's smile sparkled as she knew this was expected of her. The evening flew by as the club filled and their small group dwindled when two of the men pretexted fatigue and took a taxi back to their hotel. By now, Milduta felt she had drunk enough; she was feeling warm inside, relaxed, but still in control of the situation. Or so she believed. She wondered who of the remaining three men around their table would make a pass. She knew an offer would no doubt be forthcoming. After all, they had invested a small fortune in time and drinks in the pleasure of her company. She mentally decided she would opt for the first to come forward. No need to be choosy or have favourites.

Diplomatically, two of the men excused themselves and made for the washroom.

'So little Estonian lady,' Boris said. His tie wasn't straight, she noted. 'What about some more serious fun?'

Milduta modestly lowered her eyes.

'I don't go all the way,' she whispered. 'Or accept money. I'll be friendly with you though… you may use my mouth, and touch me if you wish.'

'Deal,' Boris nodded. 'Much healthier that way.'

His companions returned and they all downed their final drink.

It was a night of torrential rain. They all shared a cab back to the Intercontinental. None of the men even laid a tentative hand on her as they rode in silence.

They took the lift and all exited onto an endless corridor on the sixth floor. Milduta guessed they were all staying in different rooms on this same floor.

They reached the door of room 677 and Boris hunted for the key inside his coat. The two other men stood beside her. He unlocked and motioned Milduta inside as he switched the main light in the room on. The other two stepped in behind her. She turned towards the three men, as she realised what was happening.

'No,' she protested. 'Boris only.'

They laughed. The last one through the door kicked it back and set the latch.

'Come on, Mimi,' one of them said. 'Don't treat us like fools.'

She stood nailed to the ground as the realisation of her foolishness finally dawned on her.

'We know about you,' another remarked. 'The barman told us about your expertise…'

'But I've never…' she faltered.

'What?' Boris inquired.

'More than… one man,' she confessed.

'One. Three. What's the difference?' he questioned her angrily. 'You're just a cheap slut. We own you now.'

Milduta sighed heavily. Capitulated.

'My mouth only,' she pleaded.

'If you behave and please us, little Mimi,' Boris said.

'Otherwise we use your other holes, my dear.'

Her shoulders slumped.

'Strip,' they ordered.

21

So Nicky moved on.

Jack consoled himself with the fact that she had possibly been a bit too young. Blamed it on infatuation. He mourned for what could have been in a quiet, discreet way, unlike the way he had reacted so badly after Elizabeth. He reckoned you only had a given share of inner despair allotted to you in life, and it was wiser this time not to use up more of his quota. Private grief it was, then.

After all, he wasn't unattractive, he knew. He was fluent, articulate, easygoing when the occasion demanded. It had been remarked that he even displayed a witty sense of humour when the prevalent darkness didn't dominate his soul.

He knew he would meet other girls. Women.

He would surely again come across a smile that touched him deep down inside; eyes that would sparkle with laughter and recognition; the nonchalant gesture of a delicate hand brushing wind disturbed hair back; or the sound of a breathless voice over a telephone line, conveying the invisible emotions that lurked between words.

They were out there in the whole wide world. Awaiting coincidence or the right set of circumstances. He resolved to be patient. No panic, Jack. It will happen. Give time its due.

Marie-Jo shared a room with Paule in the cavernous villa in La Ciotat, by the Mediterranean, where he had been invited to spend two summer weeks in the company of a motley group of friends from the Literature Faculty. She was small and painfully thin, a picture of delicacy, and Jack's furtive eyes couldn't help catching the dark hardness of her nipples as they peered out from the underarm gap of the loose tee-shirt she wandered about the garden in. Just about a B-cup, Jack estimated, watching her tan on the beach, her small breasts buried beneath her against the hot sand, her straps loose across her back. Sadly this was years before the South of France went fashionably topless. It was an unspoken agreement between all of them that they had come down here for an undemanding break and that the friendship and camaraderie should not be spoiled by personal relationships. Jack asked her out on a date after they'd all returned to Paris and they went out twice. Her kisses lacked emotion and he never saw her breasts again. She has ash-blonde hair and loved to sport a ponytail.

Anne, the following spring, was the acknowledged girlfriend of Pascal's younger brother. Another blonde, with piercing grey eyes and a cold smile. So Jack merely lusted after her from afar, controlling raging hard-ons whenever she and her boyfriend would get the urge and leave their friends to rush upstairs to the attic bedroom for a fuck. She was a part-time lingerie model with a passion for flowers and even worked part-time at a florists, arranging bouquets, between jobs. Jack allowed her to use Alphonse's room for a few weeks when his room-mate had to return home because of an illness in his family, on the occasion Anne lost her apartment. By then, she was no longer with her boyfriend. They never actually spoke that much. Anne would blithely walk across the flat in an advanced state of undress, not realising how much she aroused him. She had long legs and her pale hair flowed down across her shoulders with all the grace of a shampoo advert. One night, Jack awoke, restless and, on the spur of the moment, slipped into the bed where Anne was sleeping. She expressed little surprise and they made love that night and then the next. Then she moved on and, when Jack barely suggested they see each other again, she grew quite contrary and explained that a couple of episodes meant nothing and she had no further desire to see him. Jack just sighed, still amazed by the depths of indifference women could sometimes demonstrate. For him, a fuck still meant something.

He met Danielle on a coach. He would use a budget airline to fly back to London.

It began with a coach service from Place de la Republique to a small airport in Beauvais, followed by a thirty-minute creaky flight over the Channel and arrival at a forlorn Sussex airport (which was no more than few sheds and a runway), and then another coach journey to Victoria station. It took nearly a whole day, but it was cheap.

Jack had spent a week back in London and it was time for the return leg to Paris, with his case full of folk albums (early Buffy St Marie, Phil Ochs and pre-Pentangle Bert Jansch) from the now long-defunct Dobell's on the Charing Cross Road. He had barely made it onto the bus in time and there were just a few seats left. He'd installed himself next to a young girl with a wild look in her eyes. He had little choice. It was either her or some rotund example of humanity some rows back.

The book she was leafing through was French and they began a conversation. Her name was Danielle, a student of some sort from the suburbs of Paris, a couple of years older than he was. So what had she been doing in London, he asked her. Oh, she'd spent a whole week in bed with this Indian guy who had incredible sexual stamina and technique and, damn it, she was exhausted. Her brazen honesty made a mark on him and he spent most of the rest of the journey with a raging hard-on, which he naturally concealed as best he could under his travelling bag. He had never come across a girl like her before. She smelt of sex, she spoke of sex, she literally breathed sex (and by now knew every page of the Kamasutra, no doubt). Just what his hormones had always dreamed of.

As the bus reached Paris and they parted, he dared ask her for her phone number. She blithely gave it to him.

He invited her to a party he was having a few weeks later. On the night, Jack would nervously glance at the door every few minutes, nervously hoping she was a woman of her word.

She arrived late, and stayed on after the other guests drifted off. Her breasts were wonderfully full. Her pubic hair was dark and curly. They fornicated like rabbits on leave.

They saw each other for six months or so, but he knew she was also seeing a score of others. She was far from exclusive with her favours, even returning to London a few times to refresh sexual matters with her Indian pal. She and Jack argued, they parted, they got together again. She left home and found a flat near the Bastille and he visited her there shortly after. She sucked him with unusual relish; they even attempted anal sex. They were relaxing in post-coital mood on the bed when the doorbell rang. She casually rose, naked, and opened the door in all her shocking nudity, pale skin and all curves. It was another boyfriend, visibly older. She invited him in and, picking up a spare blanket, moved to the next room with him, gifting Jack with an enigmatic smile. He lay there for an hour or so, seething inside, the fires of jealousy burning sharply in his gut, listening to them noisily fuck until it just got too much and he rose, dressed and ran from her apartment.

They didn't speak for a week or so. When they finally did, she threw cold water over his anger and berated him for not actually having joined them. Thus did he miss his first three-some.

They lost touch shortly after this. They only saw each other once more. He was back in London by then and she rang. She was alone and broke. He booked a hotel room. Top floor in Bloomsbury. She was on the run, possibly wanted by French police, having seduced some man and stolen his wallet. Her face looked tired. Still, they fucked. She insisted on being on top. He furtively left the room at dawn to go to his office, leaving her there asleep, with a £5 note on the bedside table. She frightened him now. Jack never heard from her again.

Did she evade jail; did she live happily ever after; would she even remember him, a hundred men or so no doubt later?

He'd never spoken to a woman on a coach since. Risky business.

At any rate, the memory of Danielle Chamaillard remained with him for a long time. His hardy, two-men-a-night woman. Another milestone in his haphazard sexual education.

Another obsession took root in his mind, of a threesome in which two men serviced the same woman. Unlike, he read in magazine articles, the majority of other men, he held no fascination, on the other hand, for witnessing two women together. Or himself with two women.

22

Milduta drifted.

Shortly after the incident with the businessmen, still full of self-loathing, and having expressed to her superiors her need for a change of horizons, she was posted for six months to a provincial outpost of the company, near Kaunas, in neighbouring Lithuania. The job was routine, something she could almost do in her sleep, but the landscapes around there were beautiful. Baltic winter at its whitest, snow as pure as paint against the regal backdrop of forests and lakes extending all the way across the immensity of the low-flying sky.

But there was also little to do at night. The men who frequented the bars here were even rougher in appearance and mentality than those she was used to seeing in Tallinn. Culture barbarians she had little truck with.

Eventually, she had to overcome her distaste and reluctantly returned to her old habits. She had no need for the men per se, but she felt the craving for their vulgar, fleshly ways and her ensuing depredation. It had now become a part of her she could not discard, however much she felt the shame to the core of her soul.

After returning to Tallinn, she left the factory and took on a succession of menial, part-time jobs in offices and the new hotels that kept on opening in the centre of town to cope with the growing interest in the country from foreign businesses. All the while, trying to figure out what to do next with her life.

Meantime, she cruised her way through the cobbled streets of the old town, with her pay-later attitude and that ever infuriating smile draped across her youthful face. The very image of insouciance and sexy innocence.

She doubted her purpose, was neither happy nor unhappy, just stranded in a lost range of emotions in-between, incapable of reaching either opposing shore. Aimless in her quiet, uncommunicative way. Running out of friends. Achieving only the superficial human contact of mouth against cock in a bid to feel alive and needed. She came to terms with her nature. If no one judged her badly for her acts of lust, why should she, after all?

A small voice inside Milduta still murmured insidiously there must be something better waiting for her around the corner, though.

She chose to ignore it and purposefully follow her meandering road to nowhere, calmly bestowing her future to the hands of fate. Everything must have a purpose, she believed. Even the bad things and the hurt.

After all, life could be worse. There was music she could dance to and close her eyes and imagine she was elsewhere, on another dance floor, with another kind of partner. There was the solace of drink, the warmth of the vodka as it warmed her guts and made her skin shine; the gin that burned her throat when she gulped it down too fast; or the smooth, velvet-like embrace of other liqueurs that blanketed her body and lowered her expectations of perfection.

And then there was the pride she somehow felt at the way men appreciated her for her looks, her eyes, her mouth, her cheerfulness, her skills with them, and she could feel them feel so good without even opening her legs for them. She seldom went with one beyond the first occasion. They came young and old, all flattering her with their carnal attentions and intentions. She knew that, in her limited way, she had the power to make them feel happy.

And when spring came again in the slow turnover of Northern seasons, she would often go with friends or a man who turned out to be kind or tender enough to warrant further intimacy (and owned a car), to the golden beaches of the Nidas Peninsula, where the sand felt as fine as silk between her fingers. Unlike other women there, she never even went topless, shy enough at her exposure in the string-like two-piece suit she had acquired at the big Cooperative store and for which she had to wax her stray curls away in a bid to avoid indecency. Many years later, when she had grown into the habit of shaving her pussy, and felt no remorse in being seen in an absolute state of nudity by men, she would still refuse to take her top off on beaches or when sunbathing. A curious contradiction at the root of her character, which had nothing to do with sex. Just natural shyness, or discretion.

On some evenings at the beach, they would all build a fire and sing and drink until the mid of night and she would sometimes agree to retreat to the nearby dunes to minister to yet another wanting man; and with her knees in the crumbling sand and her eyes fixed upwards on the crescent moon oscillating to the rhythm of her movements high up behind the square shoulders of her partner, Milduta would feel a bizarre sense of contentment. The sounds of the nearby waves lapping the shore, the distraction of the voices below on the beach and the underlying warmth of the golden soil under her, would all combine to generate a soft, fuzzy, and almost somnolent emotion of wellbeing. She loved Nidas, and when she later moved to the West, this place was what she missed most about the Baltic States and her youth.

Voraciously sucking on men's throbbing cocks under the moonlit breeze, or allowing them to touch her up with their probing fingers and sharp nails as she stretched indolently across the fine sand while her dreams of elsewhere roared inside her head, Milduta surrendered to the moment.

They wanted her to swallow as if it were an added expression of love? Fine. It was better than the rageful way some tried to impale her throat and make her gag, in a pitiful bid to establish their dominance or their virility. She would just roll the gluey liquid inside her cheek and spit the stuff out later when they had their backs turned or their eyes closed in the throes of coital joy. She sampled their taste with the tip of her tongue. Often, Milduta could almost distinguish from the flavour of their come what they had been eating or drinking earlier. A fact that amused her immensely.

But beach days never lasted and she had to return to the windowless offices and soulless factories where she had to earn a meagre living until she could afford the luxury of another visit to the Coast.

She began reading about foreign beaches in magazines: Mallorca, Ibiza, Thailand, Mexico, the Caribbean. The stuff of dreams.

23

Jack tried whores. But none of them had the power to engage his heart and their embraces were too mechanical and unfeeling. As he fucked them, he could not help wondering about their lives, about the steps in the journey that had brought them to the sordid hotel room where they opened their legs or sucked him for money. He imagined wild and outrageously romantic or graphic scenarios of their downfall or despair but he found no answers when he looked deep into their eyes. And none of them visibly appeared in the slightest bit interested in conversation.

All they wanted was for him to lower his pants – after the cash had changed hands and disappeared into their handbags – so they might quickly wash his cock in the sink before a perfunctory blow job to get him hard, after which they sheathed him in the obligatory condom, quickly followed by the woman straddling him or spread-eagling herself on her back and guiding him to her gash.

Most times, the whores of Paris kept their bras on and would tut-tut him if he attempted, in a bid for closeness, contact, to feel their breasts. There was no joy when he came, no relief, just a dull sense of frustration.

What he maybe enjoyed most about his encounters with prostitutes was walking up the usual narrow stairs right behind them, as they made their way up to the room where the two of them would couple. His eyes fixed in fascination on the latitude of their swaying arses, imagining the globes of soft flesh under the thin fabric of the tight, gaudy skirt. Later, he would seldom remember their faces or the actual sex, only the delicate shimmer of their arse as they had moved upwards to their commercial assignation.

It was to be another year or so before Jack would attempt to make love to the women he managed to seduce in anything but the missionary position, and overnight sex took on a whole different meaning as his lust raged watching a woman's rear as he entered and thrust into her. It became a vision he aspired to more than most, the supreme reward a woman could offer him, the spectacle of her arse on full display.

Not a leg or a tit man, by any measure!

He travelled the world. Developed his book-dealing business in first editions and rare, antiquarian titles, realistically aware that his writing hobby would never amount to much financially.

He prospered.

And when he found a young woman who not only touched his heart but also responded in kind, he married her.

Settled down.

Jack now attempted to banish all the female ghosts of his past on the altar of his newly found gentle form of happiness.

His wife was the friend of a friend from his Comparative Literature studies at the Sorbonne years previously. A junior doctor. They had met at a Bastille Day 14th July party. Marvelled at the fireworks shooting over the banks of the Seine and laughed at the enforced gaiety that was taking hold of the city. They slept together that same night and a few times more, followed shortly after with a quickly improvised camping holiday together to a Greek island. Jack felt comfortable with her; a state of mind that he had never enjoyed with all his previous affairs, when doubt and fear had always lurked at the back of his mind, even at the best of times. He found it pleasing that his lovemaking with her was no longer full of the rage and longing that had previously held him in its thrall. It was a revelation: simplicity and unspectacular normalcy had a virtue all of their own, far from pain and the complications of passion.

But memory is a strange beast. It remains dormant for up to decades before rearing its ugly head again when you least expect it.

The epiphany and beauty of babies briefly assuaged Jack's niggling discomfort with his new-found fate and the predictability of marriage. Initially, he didn't even realise the seeds were growing inside him. He reckoned this was just the way it was, with life, with men and women. It just wasn't like a movie; it consisted mostly of quiet moments and small joys.

So, he conveniently papered over the cracks. Or consciously ignored them.

It was for many years a good life, as lives go.

The children grew up. And Jack discovered, to his amazement, that children always disappoint to some extent. Which is how it should be, he reasoned, developing their own personalities and rebellious quirks. Wouldn't it have been boring if they had just conformed to orders and/or recommendations and turned into automatons, albeit with the sweet features they'd had as babies?

But the two boys survived all the hundred of traps that lie in wait on the road to adulthood and that was a major victory in itself, he realised. His wife and he had done their job, and not a bad one at that.

And once his mind finally retreated from the genetic fears inspired by his children's start in life, Jack looked at himself in the mirror and noticed his first grey hairs. It was over twenty years since that Ladbroke Grove evening when Pierre had first opened that hole in his heart and uncovered Catherine Guinard's treachery.

Jack realised, with little genuine surprise, as he lathered his cheeks for his daily shave, that the damn hole was still there, aching blindly, albeit to the rhythm of the slowest metronome in the world.

It slyly reminded him of all the roads never taken.

Often at night, when he would find sleep difficult, as his wife instinctively cuddled up to him in her sleep to seek his natural warmth, he would serenade himself to slumbers with a monotonous litany that endlessly conjugated all the 'what if's' of his life to date.

There were many.

Even if the following morning he seldom remembered them all, the doubts, the reservations, the recurring regrets. However, he vaguely recalled most days that in a state of half sleep each had the blurred face of a woman.

24

Milduta had struck up a friendship with a distant family cousin who supervised the laboratory practicals at the science faculty of the local university. The two girls would pair up every fortnight and spend time at the bars and on the dance floor of the student union. They both looked youthful enough to be mistaken for students. The atmosphere was more relaxed, the young men friendly and the nagging pressure for women to deliver some form of sex less commonplace. Anyway, the boys here could seldom afford endless rounds of drinks in an unsubtle bid to obligate women or weaken their resistance.

It was summer in Tallinn.

Leaves of glorious green on trees and a rare few weeks with no rain.

The jukebox was playing Spandau Ballet.

They were both sipping flat Coca-Cola. A nearby bottling plant had recently acquired the franchise and it was all the rage. Milduta found it too sweet. It was too early in the day for alcohol though.

Ekaterina was lamenting the lack of availability of decent cosmetics in the Tallinn stores. Like most women in town she relied heavily on her yearly ferry trip to Gothenburg, in Sweden, where she stocked up and dissipated much of her savings on clothes and beauty care.

'L'Oréal hair products are just the best,' she remarked to Milduta. 'Aren't they German?'

'No,' Milduta replied. 'I think they're French. I like Revlon stuff; it's from America. See my nails.'

Ekaterina glanced enviously at Milduta's long and manicured crimson nails.

'Quite decadent,' she said, with a wide, mischievous smile.

'You think so?'

'Totally.'

'You know, ten years ago it would have been unthinkable. People would have treated like me a whore for wearing this,' Milduta said, pointing to her polished nails.

'Not only the colour, but also the fact it's American.'

'Just like blue jeans...,' Ekaterina sighed. She only owned one pair of Levis, and coveted another with a passion. 'Do you ever think of America? Going there?'

A few of their friends had emigrated over the past years.

'I'm not sure,' Milduta answered. 'I'm just not attracted somehow. Sure, they have all these goods in abundance, but I hear life is so fast there, the people are so hard, it's all money money money...'

'One day, I want to go,' Ekaterina said.

Milduta nodded.

'Oh, look...' Ekaterina exclaimed.

A group of young men and women had walked in to the student union's bar. They recognised some, but four of them they had never seen before. They were foreign. You could tell not only from the clothes they were wearing, but also the way they moved. The confidence, the attitude. It was unmistakable.

'Hi,' the two young women greeted the arriving group and helped them pull up chairs, so they all now sat in a circle around the low table on which they arranged their glasses.

The newcomers were Belgian students who were visiting Estonia on an exchange programme for two months of summer classes. Their spoken Russian was halting but endearing. They were also very shy. Their Catholic University back in Belgium segregated sexes and they were unfamiliar with the camaraderie of women, and the more relaxed attitudes of the old Soviet Republics.

Milduta quickly took a liking to Serge.

She would have found it difficult to explain, had she been asked. Most of the foreign men she had previously encountered had also been from the Communist Bloc, or else from Sweden or Germany, granite-faced men with no relics of sentimentality.

Serge was different. He blushed easily, radiated gentleness and decency. He appeared genuinely interested in her, questioning endlessly about her life, her family, her country. Never even set a finger on her until the evening she boldly took his hand in hers and signified officially that she liked him.

He made Milduta's heart stagger that one beat faster. The first man to achieve the feat. He allowed her to see the future in a different light. So, she had been right all the time. Not all men were the same.

She saw him daily from then onwards, meeting up when she'd leave her office and he had completed his classes.

He was the first man Milduta invited back to the apartment she had taken over from her late grandparents. The place, with its old wooden furniture and lace curtains was her most private retreat and she had seldom even had girlfriends back. She even insisted on cooking for him on occasions. Surprised herself by how much she actually enjoyed it, busying herself in the exiguous kitchen, recreating local dishes from memory and observations of grandmother.

On their third evening she asked Serge, who had never put a foot indelicately wrong, let alone suggested anything untoward yet, to her bedroom and kissed him. His mouth still tasted of the borscht and vodka she had literally fed him earlier.

In silence, she undressed him under the soft shadow of darkness. The window to the street outside was wide open, just draped with a quilted curtain. Estonian summer still carried a chill in the air for him and Milduta marvelled at the goose bumps sprouting over his skin as she unveiled his scrawny nudity. Just a boy. Not yet fully a man, she realised. Two years younger than she was.

'Are you sure?' he asked.

'Don't worry,' she replied. 'Don't say a word.'

His cock was long and thin, somehow devoid of the rough strength and vulgarity of most of the local men's penises, she noticed. She sucked him with slow desire rising inside her own loins. He came quickly and she gratefully accepted his ejaculate in her mouth, even as he tried to withdraw from her. She gulped it down, still signifying to him that silence was required and kept on licking his glans as his whole body hiccupped epileptically in the throws of his orgasm.

'it's the first time a girl has... you know... taken me into...' he whispered, still in terrible awe of what she had done to him, with him.

Milduta said nothing and kept on sucking him with voracious appetite. Soon, he was hard again.

The second time he came was violent and he actually screamed, as the now thin and sparse drops of his come spurted towards the back of her throat.

Later, they lay in silence, hand in hand. There was little to say.

'I want to see you tomorrow,' Milduta said. 'Again.'

The following night, she relieved him orally and they fell asleep, naked together in the narrow bed, feeling their inner warmth permeate each other to their core. It was the first time Milduta had spent a whole night next to a man. She purred with delight. She felt like a woman, complete. But still, she could not summon the courage to go all the way with Serge, her sweet Belgian boy. He never asked or suggested they make love, which put her uneasy conscience at ease for the time being. He was also a good kisser, which she enjoyed.

Drifting off into the lands of his sleep, with his shallow breath at her side punctuating her rambling thoughts, Milduta swore to herself that this was the first man she would allow herself to be fucked by.

Soon.

25

As summer ended, Serge returned to Belgium to resume his final year of studies there. He was hoping to become an interpreter at the Common Market headquarters in the Berlemont. He already spoke English and German. The course in Russian had been planned to add a further minor credit to his CV and was not vital to his prospects. He and Milduta had mostly communicated in English anyway, as he had difficulties understanding everything she said since Russian was heavily accented because of its Baltic origins.

Their parting at the main railway station was subdued. She refused to cry; she disliked the idea of public scenes of grief or affection.

They began a fragile correspondence, affected by their respective lack of grammar and precision of vocabulary and the poor service of the Tallinn postal authorities, who appeared to have a knack for losing or unseemly delaying mail, particularly of foreign origin.

Milduta resolved to improve her communication skills and enrolled in evening classes in English, two nights a week at the Polytechnic.

The older men who also participated in the course openly lusted over her but she quickly informed them she now had a foreign boyfriend, and was spoken for. Anyway, most of them were married and only sought a bit on the side, she knew.

The classes were free, so Milduta was also economising by not going out to the usual bars she frequented. She was determined to save enough to get a visa and a flight to somewhere in the West where she would see Serge again.

Nebulously, she planned her future.

In the meantime, she would still visit the dance clubs or union dances on Saturday nights, consort with men and, if they insisted, go down on her knees and perfunctorily take their cocks in her mouth. It meant nothing, she consoled herself. She had promised herself, her whole body, her soul, her unbroken hymen to gentle Serge from Ghent.

What she did now, she justified to herself, was just simple commerce, a concession to Estonian reality. So she complied with detachment, always warning the predatory and partly inebriated men who sought her services what her limits were, what she would do to them and warned them she would no way go one single, sexual step beyond.

Faced with her stubborn determination, they usually demurred with little protest. After all, they knew her reputation as a great little cocksucker already and a blow job from a fresh-looking and pretty young girl was not to be dismissed, since most working men in town had to do the deed with the whores in the port, most of whom sported stained teeth or no teeth at all.

To help put money aside, Milduta also volunteered for extra hours at her office, where they were beginning to computerise the accounts system but still operated the previous system in tandem for six months to iron out all possible problems. The opportunity suited her well.

Serge had written, shortly after Christmas, that he wanted them to spend the next summer together, after he had graduated. When he could find the time, he was also working part time at the offices of an uncle who had a law firm, slowly accumulating the money they would need for their holiday. They discussed where they might go. His early suggestion of driving across America was not to her liking. She would rather spend the time on a beach, she replied. Somewhere hot and tropical.

'I like sand to be fine, and we two spend very lazy time in

our arms together,' Milduta wrote back. 'Juss you and me. Maybe you find deserted island somewhere?'

He agreed and promised to investigate the possibilities. Reminded her in a PS that he loved her truly with all his heart.

Never before had a man confessed to be in love with her. Milduta was transformed. Even stayed away from Saturday night clubs for a few weeks, until the fleshly cravings inside got the better of her.

'When we meet, you be my first man,' she painstakingly typed with two fingers on the big Olivetti at her office. 'We make love. I not be virgin any more for you. Will be wonderful, my sweetie.'

He asked her whether she also had feelings for him.

'I love you too,' Milduta replied. 'Je t'aime, ma cheri.'

He corrected her: 'I'm a man, so you should write "mon cheri". But it does not matter, my lovely Mimi.'

In the spring, she found a splendid black bikini, cut high. It would be perfect for their tropical beach, Milduta decreed, even though it showed a lot of her white arse. But she knew that Serge would like it, and her.

Finally, back in Belgium, Serge managed to book the ideal vacation. They would go to a beach in the south of Thailand. Milduta thought it sounded wonderfully exotic and readily agreed. They would have their own individual small hut on the beach, a short distance from the hotel's main building. He sent her a copy of the travel brochure with various colour photographs of the place. It looked like paradise.

Because the holiday had been a cancellation, hence its bargain price, they would have to catch a plane out to Thailand from London, in England. Serge assured her he would send her the money for the flight to London by Western Union the following month. Let her spend the money she had saved so far on nice summer clothes, he wrote. Her roubles wouldn't convert into much Western currency, she knew, so his generosity was sadly necessary. However, she knew that he also found money hard to come by, between studies for his final exams and revision time.

She arranged to vacate her grandparents' old flat just before the summer, camping for a couple of weeks on a work acquaintance's sofa, and storing her few worthwhile belongings in a girlfriend's cellar. The couple who had taken over the flat had paid her a hundred dollars in cash. Her small nest egg.

She acquired the plane ticket to London. At first she thought she would only get a one-way ticket, as she believed she would never return to Tallinn, but the return fare cost barely a little more, for reasons she couldn't fathom. Maybe a contingency, she reckoned. She resigned from her job, mercilessly culled her clothes for the trip and was consumed by impatience.

On July 1st, symbolically for Milduta the first day of her summer, her brother dropped her at the airport.

26

'Would you like to come up to my room?' Jack tentatively asked. Neither hoping for nor expecting a positive answer.

'Sure.'

He had been having a meal alone in the old part of town in Athens, and had somehow got into a conversation with a young American woman sitting at table opposite. They had left the restaurant together and shared a few drinks in a nearby taverna. She was on the final week of a six-month tour of Europe and was returning to Cedar Rapids a few days later. She just felt lonely that night and appreciated the company. So did Jack, who was no great fan of the Greek capital.

Blushing deeply, she had confessed to something of an extreme sexual encounter she had enjoyed in Turkey weeks earlier, where her local lover had insisted she perform with another man in his presence. Under duress she had agreed, fearing for her safety, but maybe felt that by revealing her shame to a stranger she could purge some of its memories.

Jack lent a sympathetic ear. He had always been a good listener.

'Just fuck me. No need for words,' she had said after their first kiss in his hotel bedroom.

It was the first time he had been unfaithful to his wife.

'Do me doggie style,' she had asked him, after they had hurriedly undressed. She had bruises across her rump and stomach, he noticed. He assumed they had originated in Turkey. Her body was slight, almost scrawny, her stomach flat and hard like a washing board, her skin uniformly pale. She had evidently not spent long in the sun in her Mediterranean travels.

He positioned himself behind her as she knelt on the edge of the bed and raised her rear to his level.

He slammed into her, almost with rage and plowed her with all the energy and frustration he had been accumulating inside for some years now. As he fucked her, he could hear her cry softly.

'It's OK,' she protested when he queried this, and angrily begged him to be harder and rougher with her.

With every thrust into her, he could not help being transfixed by the darker corolla of her arse hole, winking at him, dilating a little with his repeated movements below in her cunt.

Later, after she'd had a few cigarettes, he quickly got hard again with surprising ease and had anal sex with her. An act he had often thought of but never tried properly (Danielle had actually been willing but proven too tight, even with improvised lubrication).

She left his room at six in the morning to return to her own hotel, a cheaper place on the other side of Metaxas Square. He offered to escort her there or at least walk down to the lobby and see her off, but she declined.

They had not even exchanged addresses or telephone numbers and within a few weeks Jack's mind even blanked out the memory of her name, surprised as he was that he didn't feel guilty at what had occurred.

If his first affair, albeit brief, had been unplanned, later encounters were more premeditated as he discovered to his surprise that he had an effortless talent for attracting other women. Maybe it was his status as a theoretically married man, his aloof attitude, which many read mistakenly as arrogance, or the fact he stood out from the crowd, an eternal anti-conformist whose dark side could be guessed at with ease for those with practised eyes.

There was a woman he had gently lusted after at his office. They met again for after-hours drinks a few months after she had moved to another company, and drifted into the affair he proposed.

Next, a late-night encounter at a trade fair, where he and another journalist had paired off with two delegates from Oregon they had come across at the taxi stand and agreed to share a ride with. Ironically, his friend had not passed first base, while Jack soon had the canary-yellow skirt off the young woman in a thrice and slept with her for the following three nights of the fair. She was convenient, if a little passive in her embraces, he found. They would meet at the fair for each of the following three years and bed each other out of habit.

The only guilt Jack experienced with these other women was just the fact he felt no real emotions toward them as they offered him their bodies.

Maybe the next one would come to mean something, he kept on hoping. So there was always another to present her pretty head around the corner when Jack least expected her to, but the whole rigmarole of illicit sex and adultery just became too easy, too empty and meaningless.

The satisfactions of sex were just so transitory, never lasted long beyond the short-circuit in his synapses or the time it took for the sweat to dry against his skin.

Jack was disappointed with life. There was nothing threatening about this. He certainly was unlikely to ever conceive of suicide again after the fiasco with Elizabeth, no fear. So he bore his cross stoically, believing by now that this was all there was to life and that he had maybe read too many books or seen to many movies that promised more, things which just didn't exist in all likelihood.

Or possibly Jack just didn't understand anything about this alien concept of happiness.

Some class he had possibly missed out on school, because of flu or some now-forgotten ailment, he kidded himself.

27

Her flight landed at Gatwick airport, south of London.

It was mid afternoon.

Serge had arrived there an hour earlier from Zaventem, Brussels and stood there by the exit from the customs and immigration zone, a large rucksack by his side. He smiled blissfully as Milduta made her way towards him through the milling crowd of visiting Estonians overloaded with old cardboard cases and plastic bags full of vodka bottles and caviar tins for their relatives abroad – a better fare than hard currency. Milduta had done likewise, but restricted herself to the two litres of alcohol she assumed was the rule, ignorant of the fact that the customs officers kept a blind, indulgent eye when it came to flights from Eastern Europe.

He raised his arms to greet her.

Milduta's first impression of Serge, after almost a year apart, as she approached him, manoeuvring herself through the throng of passengers and greeters, was that he wasn't quite as tall as she remembered. Also, that wide-open smile of his struck her as somewhat silly. Not kindness but naivety. He took her into his arms. Memory was a strange thing, she pondered.

The tweed jacket he wore fitted badly and the collar of his blue shirt had seen better days.

His light brown hair hung limply, his parting askew.

'You look lovely,' he said, after letting her go, and examining her.

'Thanks,' was the only response she could conjure.

She was just wearing jeans and a white, short-sleeved tee-shirt, just comfortable travelling things. No need to get her better clothes unnecessarily creased this early in the trip, she had reckoned.

'So...'

'So, here we are. Together. Oh, Mimi, it's going to be wonderful, you just see. Come, let me take your case.'

He juggled the rucksack and the large leather holdall that had been her grandfather's, and led her across the airport floor. She followed impassively. Somehow she now didn't quite know what to say any more, after rehearsing for ten months all the words and feelings she had been painfully storing in her mind for this day.

They caught the train to Victoria Station, holding hands as they sat close to each other in the open carriage in a simulacrum of tenderness, as Serge babbled on about their forthcoming holiday in Thailand. The flight out to Bangkok did not depart until midday the following day from Heathrow, London's other airport, so they would be staying in London itself that night. He had managed to book them a hotel in the centre of town. Milduta watched the English countryside roll by outside the train window. It was greener than back home, but fields were fields and cows were cows. Suddenly, the world felt smaller.

The sky had turned to grey and evening already beckoned by the time they reached Bloomsbury and the streets surrounding the British Museum and located their hotel, in the warren of small, identical streets lined with budget hotels. The room they were given was small, the bed narrow and the tap by the sink dripped slowly, and Milduta failed to tighten it enough to halt the insidious sound of the leaking water. The carpet was frayed at the edges, and the door to the lone cupboard didn't close properly.

Oblivious to the setting, Serge held her tightly against him, once they had pushed their cases into a corner of the room, and kissed her with undisguised passion, his tongue digging wetly inside her mouth. Milduta tasted the tobacco on his breath. Back home, it had not bothered her.

She slowly detached herself from him.

'I'm hungry,' she said.

'We'll go find something to eat then,' Serge reacted.

They found a nearby bar and had great hamburgers, chips and coffee.

Milduta was about to suggest they walk towards London's bright lights and explore this new city, but Serge said, 'I want you' before she could suggest it and they walked back to their hotel room.

She lost her virginity in Bloomsbury that evening.

After all, she had agreed to gift the Belgian boy with her soul and there was no turning back now.

They undressed. The English summer was no warmer than Tallinn and she had insisted they keep the window slightly ajar because of his cigarette smoking.

They had slipped under the covers, both shivering, and welcomed the contact of skin against skin in a bid for warmth. His hands roamed all over her uncovered body and Milduta closed her eyes and tried to respond. He gently twisted her nipples, and she felt a twinge of pain instead of pleasure. His fingers continued downwards and reached her cunt, probed the stickiness of her opening, but she was still relatively dry. In a bid to express her lust, under the cover, she extended her hand and sought his cock. He was already rock hard. She caressed him. Serge moaned softly.

Their limbs tangled as they embraced, adjusting their bodies to the confines of the narrow bed which could barely contain the two of them, let alone their motion and constant adjustments as they familiarised themselves with each other's shape and intimacies.

His arm caught uncomfortably under hers in the throws of a deep kiss, their tongues mingling freely, Serge moved and, for just a second or less, his lingering finger grazed her anus. Milduta jumped. It had been unwelcome, like a jolt of electricity, and taken her breath away. Reminding her of how little control she had over her own body and its reactions.

Serge mistook her reaction.

'Do you want to? Now?' he inquired.

'OK,' Milduta agreed. There was no point in delaying the inevitable.

There was no need to use her mouth on him. His long, thin cock already had the consistency of wood. He slipped a condom on. It was something she had insisted on.

He moved on top of her and she widened the angle between her legs.

'You really want?' he asked.

'Yes,' she answered.

He positioned himself at the threshold of her opening and slowly began to introduce his member into her. But they were both nervous and he failed to progress beyond his mushroom-like head as Milduta automatically tightened and barred his way and he was too shy, or gentle, to force her last defence.

'Maybe another way; another position.'

They switched.

He lay back, his cock jutting upwards like a flagpole and Milduta squatted above him and gradually lowered herself onto him. She had read about this in *The Joy of Sex*. She was tight. Nerves, lack of experience, lack of genuine feelings also. Once again, the head breached her lips and felt resistance. Milduta bit her lips and forced herself down, impaling herself on him in one frenzied movement, and tore herself open. It hurt. Felt like an alien object inside her gut, invading her, filling her, stretching her to previously unthought-of limits. Serge began thrusting upwards into her insides as she settled her rear on his thighs and the pain began to ebb ever so slowly.

She bled profusely that first time, relieved to know they would not be spending a second night in the hotel room and would not have to confront the maid or the staff at the reception desk after the spreading stain on the white sheet had been discovered. As she expected for the first time, after all she had researched the subject for some years now, she felt no pleasure from the act.

The water from the tap when she washed herself clean afterwards was tepid. She watched with awed fascination the mixture of blood and come slide down the plughole.

Serge had come quickly after her hymen had torn.

As she lay against the now snoring young man, she realised she no longer felt any affinity with him.

He had already become a stranger.

28

Jack dreamed of death.

The children were peacefully asleep in their rooms upstairs, for once both under the family roof at the same time.

His wife was out on call.

The house was silent around him.

Even the living sounds of the dishwasher and the dozing fridge had moved into another dimension of forgetfulness.

He gloomily dreamed of death in dark alleys, in western shootouts with blood seeping like ketchup from gaping wounds, of slow lingering deaths in soiled, sick beds, where all hope has flown.

The images he had witnessed earlier this evening on the television screen of the mass graves of the Yugoslavian conflict had reminded him of the bleak documentaries and black-and-white photographs of the concentration camps of WWII and the broken bodies of Jews piled high for the funeral pyre. Of course, he was Jewish himself, although he had seldom felt any sense of belonging to his race. His upbringing had been too liberal and scattershot. As he often joked with women he knew, the most Jewish part of him was his circumcised penis, as he had never even had the curiosity to set foot inside a synagogue for worship.

He had reached what was likely to be the midpoint of his life and was attempting a balance sheet of achievements and failures.

His business was going well and now functioned on its own momentum. His initial dreams of a writing career had floundered on the rocks of life's realities. Time had been at a premium and he knew all too well that he never had the true determination and spirit of self-sacrifice to succeed.

Worse was the inner knowledge of the fact he had nothing of value to say. His ideas were derivative and he basically harboured no ambition to change the world or set it to rights. The occasional stories he still penned had little originality or conviction. Just vignettes, tales about other people, imaginary men and women, about the interaction between the sexes and how emotions ruled lives and, more often than not, ruined them. All this cleverly wrapped around the comfortable cloak of adventures on other planets or fantasy dimensions.

Jack's tales did not predict the future, nor use the canvas of lands of never to oppose the fundamentals of good and evil, as his superiors in the writing game did with unequalled verve and elegance.

He was strictly small league.

And knew his place.

He still did columns or opinion pieces for magazines or trade journals, but it was the sort of writing he could churn out with no superfluous effort. Evidence of a lesser form of talent, he knew.

His dreams were of other things than the transience of fame.

Of women, past and future.

His fantasy life was rich and wonderfully obscene; daydreams of outrageous romanticism that would have better fit into terrible medieval legends, albeit somewhat more explicit. But he knew that the persistence of these impossible dreams was harming his soul, as another part of his brain knew all too well how improbable these tales of amour fou happened to be. A delusion.

He counted women past on his fingers, often forgetting one or the other one-night stand in the process, causing him to list them on the first piece of paper he could lay his hands on. Which he quickly had to destroy thereafter. The ones he had slept with, first. Those he had coveted from afar next. Those who had meant something or some who hadn't but whom he had used. Was he a bad man for having done this?

Was he a good man at heart?

He held no answers.

But tonight, the tenacious dreams persisted, trailing desire in their wake, allowing low, grey clouds to settle over his mind.

He remembered how the cancer had eaten away at his mother's insides and how he never visited her grave any more, even though the cemetery was just three miles away from where he now lived. Out of fear.

He wondered what other people made of him?

He knew he could turn the charm on and off at will, could easily make a woman smile and get into bed with him. A skill he would have loved to have had when he had still been younger and less cynical.

But at the end of the day, Jack felt he was at the helm of his own life on automatic pilot, still seeking answers, wanting more than he possessed already. A greedy man who always hoped for more.

29

As both Serge and the travel brochure had promised, the beach, a few miles east of Phuket, was a sheer vision of paradise. They reached it following a long, dusty journey by bus from Bangkok.

Of course, both Serge and Milduta had seen images of tropical resorts before, but the reality was otherwise. The photographs and films didn't factor in the oppressive but liberating heat, the fragrant smell of spices suspended in the air and the sheer sense of relief that the arrival in such an oasis of beauty represented after the endless flight from London, and the no less tiresome drive from the Thai capital on rickety roads full of potholes, and the somnolent proximity of other backpackers packed onto the seats and into the aisles of the coastal bus like sardines.

On arrival, Milduta was relieved to see the majority of the young Western backpackers retreat to other guesthouses.

Their hotel seemed to attract a better class of traveller, she noted.

She might well be from an Eastern European backwater, but that didn't mean she should accept lesser standards of comfort, Milduta knew.

That first night in Thailand, she slept like a log. Serge had perfunctorily mounted her before they had fallen asleep but she had felt little, her whole body already switched off from the rigours of the journey. When she finally woke the following day, it was past midday and Serge had left a note for her warning her he had gone to the beach and didn't wish to disturb her. Said she looked like an angel when she slept. Filling the rest of the sheet of paper with lines of x x x to signify his love.

It had been a night full of bizarre dreams she could no longer remember.

Her mouth was dry and she sipped from the bottle of Evian by the side of the bed. The water was unpleasantly warm.

She was grateful he was no longer by her side and spent an extra hour just relaxing, sprawling indolently in the luxury of the bed and the low-ceilinged hut, enjoying the privacy; the ceiling fan buzzed gently as it repeated its endless revolutions above her. She was acutely conscious of the fact that Tallinn and her previous life were now a world away. She could feel her gash was still leaking a little and angrily realised that Serge had not used a condom when he'd penetrated her the night before. She had been too tired to even note the fact. The bastard!

Milduta rose lazily and walked to the bathroom to wash. There was still a bit of blood seeping from her.

She lowered the shaving mirror fixed to the bathroom wall and contemplated her cunt in the heavy magnification. Her labia were still a bit puffy and swollen, but apart from that it looked no different from before London. There was nothing external to specifically indicate she was now a fully fledged woman. Milduta sighed.

Wandering naked across the floor of the hut she felt a wonderful sense of liberation. She peered through the window and saw the beach outside unroll all the way to the horizon over the emerald expanse of the sea. She noticed Serge, apparently asleep in the sun, his back already turning pink, the pages of his paperback fluttering in the breeze. Further down the beach were other people, scattered here and there at random. She did a double take: many of them were nude. Both men and women. Sounds of laughter reached her.

Serge had bought her a new bikini suit in the duty-free zone at Gatwick airport, a modest orange outfit she had taken a liking to. She had surprised him when she had revealed she only had one bathing suit.

Which to wear today, she wondered?

She wasn't about to go nude, in spite of the environment, she decided. Just wasn't in her, she knew.

Milduta was determined to enjoy her holiday. She had no wish to begin thinking of tomorrow, what would happen after the summer months. Whatever occurred would be determined by fate, she philosophically decided. She slipped the bikini on and made her way to the beach, initially burning the soles of her feet in the midday sand as she had forgotten her sandals.

The summer raced by and she made the best of it, in spite of the fact her stomach found itself at loggerheads with the local food and she suffered from acute constipation one day out of two on average, which made her feel particularly bloated and totally unsexy.

Now that she had given herself to Serge, his sexual appetites were relentless and he seemed to want to fuck her every morning, afternoon and night. His desire never tired.

Milduta no longer felt any pain during the act having, through initial trial and now constant experience, been stretched enough to accommodate his cock inside her. Often, as she closed her eyes under his thrusts, she would mischievously picture the cocks of some of the other men who moved unfettered across the beach and imagine how differently they would have felt, investing her insides, forcing her wide and wantonly. Actually, it was the only way she could approach pleasure whilst in Serge's embrace. He had little meaningful conversation bar his declarations of puppy love eternal and his annoying habit of wishing to hear how well he had satisfied her after every fuck. The lying came easy to Milduta.

He was also a creature of habit, always scorning her mild, cheeky suggestions they fuck maybe elsewhere than in bed for a change; in the sand outside or the hotel's pool after dark when there was no supervision or, an acute fantasy of hers as she grew used to gaining her pleasure there manually while he was away reading his law books on the beach, in the bathtub. The mere idea seemed to horrify him.

But when they were in the room, he was always the one to initiate sex. At the end of their first week together by the beach, her cunt was sore, inside and outside, from the pounding she had to submit to. By now, she consoled herself with the fact that his penis was relatively thin and unlike some of the others she had known previously or admired in full display on the nude beach. The German men were wondrously if scaringly thick, she had noted. She could only speculate at their girth when erect.

But Milduta knew that the continuous sex with Serge was also the price she had agreed to pay for this holiday. He was harmless, she knew, but she had quickly come to the conclusion she had lost any feelings she had ever had for him. He appeared happy, unconcerned that he had blown all his savings on her and this tropical idyll.

She was aware that she was using him, but the thought came easy. There was little guilt involved. After all, he was liberally using her body. Once again it came down to an impersonal transaction involving supply and demand. It was that simple.

He no longer even required blow jobs, ever content to fuck her in the missionary position.

Anything to keep him happy.

So be it.

30

Jack met Edwina at a professional function in the provinces; one of those formal black-tie and lukewarm champagne evenings where the company he had to keep bored him to high heaven and he kept on the look-out for plausible excuses to leave early. His wife, who had the flu, had been unable to join him. The mood he was in, he would have been short-tempered with her anyway, as he was far too often of late, much to his ulterior guilt.

Edwina was tall, blonde of course, and also married. Although he did not notice the ring on her finger until their second meeting.

They initially exchanged polite conversation about the weather, the poor financial health of the British public library system or whatever had been in the newspaper headlines that week, but the subtitles below their dialogue were already rampant with lust.

Something about her. The way she stood, how she averted her eyes just a second too late when he gazed at her pale face, the tone of her voice, the obvious impatience she shared with him about their surroundings and company.

They were unable to sit together, or surreptitiously swap place names at the formal banquet and awards ceremony that concluded the evening, having been allocated separate tables.

'Where do you live? London, I assume?'

'Yes. South of the river.'

'Do you need a lift later?'

'I'd already made arrangements, but thank you. It's kind.'

'Pity. The drive down the M1 can be so tedious. Would have been nice to have company.'

'Maybe another time?'

A brief silence while the ambulating waitress filled their glasses again.

'Strange that we've never met before.'

'Yes, it is.'

Jack breathed a deep sigh. Edwina kept on looking at him, as if she expected him to say something more, delaying her short journey to the dinner table where she had been seated. Most of the other guests had already settled down. He finally spoke.

'I'd like to see you again.'

She didn't flinch. The shadow of a smile moved across her lipstick.

'Me too,' she answered.

She handed him her business card.

'It's a direct line.'

The sex on their first time in bed raged out of control, as if both of them had been waiting for this day all their lives. It took them both by surprise. It was full of rage, undiluted hunger, vulgar and tender, wild and meaningful, a throwback to the primeval sources of animal desire. No sooner had they kissed with unabashed greed as the door to the hotel room slammed behind them that she whispered in his ear 'I want you inside me, now...' and they didn't emerge from their red fog until four hours later, both out of breath, out of words and their mind prey to such unexpected turmoil they could never have imagined previously.

Within instants, as the silence settled and they couldn't take their eyes off each other, still coated with sweat, the sheets tangled and stained beneath and across them, the lust they had unleashed turned, against their better judgement, into a surfeit of affection.

Edwina bent over and began licking his cock, still coated with her juices.

'It's not clean,' Jack protested mildly.

'So?' was her only form of response as she took all of him into the hollow of her cheeks and he felt the hardness of his desire impossibly awaken again.

For the first time since as far back as he could remember, Jack felt fulfilled and momentarily lost contact with the emptiness inside that had been laying siege to his guts.

They meet on every possible occasion when dual alibis can plausibly be arranged. It proves far from easy as a dedicated, adulterous relationship is a killer to organise properly and so much more problematic an enterprise than instinctive one-night stands or spur-of-the-moment drunken fucks against night walls in dark places.

They steal lunch breaks, pretext after-hour meetings, invent weekend excuses to meet and sleep together. Not that they get much sleeping done once they have torn each other's clothes off.

They make love on hard floors, tables and in hotel bathtubs. The whole world is pregnant with possibilities as they improvise wildly in underground car parks, no doubt in full view of the ever-present security cameras and chuckling observers. They have no shame. They finger each other to pleasure in the darkness of cinemas, and the front rows where few others venture. They fuck in his car, in motorway rest zones, too impatient to reach the hotel booked further up the road, or even while he is still driving as she sits on him and enjoys the thrust of his penis grazing her cervix with every new bump of the country road they are moving down. They are indefatigable and joyous. Slaves to their bodies.

He ties her hands and, in shock, she flushes deep crimson with delight. No man has ever restrained her before. She imagines she is a slave, like in an Anne Rice s/m novel.

He breaches her sphincter ring with two and then three fingers and she uncontrollably squirms and moans under his invasive touch like a woman possessed, and he speaks softly into her ear of all the other abominable things he wishes to do to her.

'Yes,' Edwina sighs, on the very edge of orgasm. 'Yes. I want you to use me, use me, and use me again…'

Jack makes plans.

He wants to take her to Cap d'Agde, New York, Barcelona, Bangkok. Even as they exhaust his wildest fantasies, he conjures up more fantasies, involving Edwina in alien places where her beauty, her thin pallor, will shine like a pearl emerging from its shell.

He promises her the world and more.

He loves to watch the scarlet pool of her orgasmic flush spread from her cheeks to her chest while she lies on the bed, still dripping with his juices, in the penumbra of the anonymous rooms they are forced to use; the strong smell of their exertions and the echo of their whispered obscenities still hanging like a stain in the air while they catch their breath.

He adores the gentle but intrusive vaginal farts that punctuate the sound of their fucking as his cock somehow extends deeper and deeper into her vagina and displaces small pockets of air inside her boiling innards; she blushes apologetically when this happens and her embarrassment is just another spur to his overflow of love for her.

Jack is reborn.

31

On the tedious journey back from Thailand, Milduta only had limited transit time at Gatwick airport before catching her connection to Tallinn on a budget airline flight. Serge had planned to stay in London a few extra days to meet some local lawyers his uncle had provided him introductions to, with a view to securing a job in the Brussels office of a British legal firm.

Milduta, all tanned and resplendent from her two months away soaking up the Thai sun, sleepwalked back into her old job and, reluctant to seek new permanent accommodation in earnest, sub-let a small, airless bedroom in the flat of a remote acquaintance of her brother's.

She was determined not to stick around too long in her native Estonia.

She would return to the West, she knew, whatever it took.

In the meantime, after so many weeks of being fucked by the same cock, she craves the experience of different men.

She resumes her routine of bestowing her blow jobs at the local dance halls to her escorts for the evening. One Saturday night in October, she drinks far too much after a works party, lowers her resistance and lets a Polish sailor fuck her roughly in the tunnel near the railway station.

'Want your pussy, girl, not your mouth,' he says, reacting angrily to her initial proposal.

He has no manners to speak of, trips her over the boot of an abandoned Skoda left there to rot, tears her panties off and impales her with one forward thrust and repeatedly spanks her arse as he pushes deeper and deeper into her. Had he stayed hard just a minute or so longer, she would even have come, something she has yet to achieve with a man.

Serge writes early in the fall, asking her to come join him Belgium for the Christmas season. He has told his parents all about her and they are keen to meet her. He will, naturally, send her a plane ticket and supply the official consular invitation so she might obtain an exit visa.

Milduta agrees to the trip. His parents take a shine to her, as do his two sisters; she is pretty, well spoken, and has an adorable accent when she talks to them in English. And even though her Baltic background is far from their ideal, they recognise she is a better bet than some of the rough-and-tumble local girls their son had earlier gone out with. The lesser, and much more demure and presentable, of two evils. For the sake of propriety, she sleeps in the spare room. On a couple of occasions, Serge joins her there late at night when the rest of the household is asleep, but Milduta pretexts her period and doesn't grant him sex.

'It doesn't matter,' he mildly protests. 'We'll just be more careful, you know.'

'No,' Milduta answers. 'I just don't like the idea of sex when I am... dirty down there, you see.'

On Christmas Eve, she and Serge have an invitation to a large celebratory dinner with friends of his from the local Law Faculty. Most of the erstwhile students are local, but there are also a handful of Dutch men and women present who had attended the same classes or lectured there. Serge introduces her to Henk, who had been a tutor of his on commercial jurisprudence some years previously. Henk has a beard, now works for a business magazine catering to the shipping industry, and is ten years older than Milduta.

They all drink too much.

At midnight, after the traditional, if clumsy, wet kiss from Serge on the stroke of the hour, Milduta finds herself facing the lean Dutchman.

'Don't I get a kiss too?' he winks at her.

She looks back. Serge is affectionately embracing his other friends.

She moves closer to Henk.

An hour later, Milduta leaves the party with him and sleeps with him.

The following day, Henk presents himself at the two-storeyed building where Serge and his parents lived, apologises unconvincingly on her behalf and picks up her suitcase and clothes. She follows him back to London just before the turn of the year. He owns a small house near a canal, just a half-hour's drive from Amsterdam. He is very dominant. Which is fine with her; she likes the fact he takes all the decisions and that her fate is no longer so completely in her own hands. He also owns a small wooden barge which he uses in summer to accompany tourists on the canals of the region. He hopes that this business will one day develop and allow him to give up his other job. His beard tickles but she appreciates that he usually goes down on her, eating her cunt with undisguised appetite as a prelude to mounting her. She finds she can come easily when he does that, long before he even enters her. The later hydraulics add little further sensation to the degrees of her pleasure, although she realises it's a necessary part of his sexual menu.

His cock is paler than Serge's but much thicker, its mush-room head more pink than purple in shade, once she had delicately unrolled the tight foreskin and revealed it

She knows nothing about his past. She doesn't ask him any questions. She is living with him, isn't that enough?

Milduta just refuses to indulge in sentimentality.

There are days when Henk is good company, generous, expansive; then there are other days when he is silent and morose. Milduta accepts the good with the bad. She begins to grapple with the Dutch language and its guttural inflections.

Six months later, Milduta is pregnant by Henk. She even recalls with utter precision the occasion it happened. They had argued badly that day, about money and their lack of it, and ended up drinking that awful juniper alcohol he was inordinately fond of. She was unsteadily climbing the stairs to their bedroom on the upper floor when he had followed her and brusquely pulled her down over the stair steps, reached for her skirt and angrily parted her legs and thrust himself into her, while manically pulling her long hair backwards until it really hurt. Fortunately, he'd come quickly. The next morning, she'd found bruises all across her ribs and stomach where the weight of his heavier body had ground her cruelly into the stairs as he roughly took his pleasure from her passive body.

After she announced her pregnancy to him, he never even manifested any satisfaction, and would always refer to their forthcoming child as specifically hers. From that day onwards, and throughout the following five months or so until she was too big, he refused to make love to her vaginally, and used the pregnancy as an excuse to fuck her repeatedly in the arse, which she disliked intensely.

But Milduta was resolute. She wanted this baby more than anything, so she kept her silence and allowed Henk, who by now had lost his job at the trade paper and was trying his luck as a ship chandler, to dominate and use her.

If it was a girl, she had decided she would be called Aida, the opera-inspired name of her friend who had died in childbirth the previous year.

32

Jack's liaison with Edwina ended as abruptly as it had begun. One night she had whispered softly in his ears how much she desired him and how no man before had satisfied her so intensely, and then four days later she had suggested, averting her eyes as she broke the news to him, that they not see each other for a few months. Calm things down. Get the relationship into some form of perspective. He sadly knew how to translate this hopeless request.

Within days, despite his pleas and frantic letters, she had broken off all communication within him and stayed with her dull marriage.

He never quite figured out what had happened. He assumed her husband had discovered about the affair and given her an ultimatum. Whatever the cause for her sudden change of heart, it no longer mattered. She had chosen between the lesser of two evils, he reckoned, and Jack was left holding the pieces.

He had never even seen the end coming. Or maybe he had intentionally misread all the earlier signs. The bitter tears on the occasion she slipped up on her alibi and missed a telephone call from her husband, and assumed he would easily put two and two together and throw her out of their home. The call had nothing to do with the affair, just some mundane matter she'd well forgotten. Or the remote look in her grey eyes whenever Jack would describe the foreign cities he wished to take her to some forthcoming day. Or again, her nervous insistence on their always patronising bars and hotels where none of their common acquaintances were ever likely to chance upon them.

Jack drowned his abysmal sorrow by working every hour of the following weeks in a bid to erase the still scarred memories of Edwina and listening through the night to melancholy music with the volume turned to a maximum, imagining a lavish and sad soundtrack for his small-time tragedy.

And again he dreamed of death.

The grief quickly turned to anger, blithely skipping the other five, or was it six, prescribed stages in the theoretical book of sorrow.

So Jack dreamed of Edwina's death in a thousand-and-one circumstances. Trivial accidents, horrific catastrophes man-made and natural, self-inflicted, premeditated; he pictured her as a victim of fate, she who must die. Imagined the wounds, the violations, the last agonising minutes as she relived her whole life in the flash of a final second, realising how much she had missed when she rejected him, of course. Then his warped sense of revenge stepped backwards and constructed complete and elaborate scenarios leading to her demise. Stories full of semen and fury and self-loathing, in which her cold heart turned to ice as he remembered her and interpreted anew every one of their meetings, embraces and conversations, seeking the clues to her ultimate decision and, unilaterally punishing her with the wrath of his love.

Jack felt for some time still to come that he would rather she was dead than no longer his.

Then came the turn to conceive yet more extravagant story lines to dispose of her cuckold of a husband, whom he hated more than hate itself by virtue of his sheer existence.

And, at random moments of abjection, he would even dream briefly of the passing of his own wife. An exotic infection caught during her hospital rounds; a car accident on the way to an emergency call; a stroke; an allergy to a new species of fruit that would cull her within minutes of ingestion.

Just dreams.

Did he even truly wish for any of these awful desires to become reality? Not really. It was merely a by-product of the rage seething inside him, the bitterness that consumed him.

A peculiar way of exorcising the recent events and the loss of tousle-haired Edwina.

And, naturally, all these thoughts of revenge came to nothing.

Jack was quite aware he was too much of a coward to do anything about the situation. Not that any action he could take was likely to change the past anyway. Life wasn't a science-fiction novel. Not even in the year 1984!

Maybe he was just a sexual romantic who'd seen too many movies and felt time and time again that every life, every relationship, required a soundtrack?

Or a disgusting, self-deluded pornographer, who believed that the shocking intimacy of every act of sexual excess could attain sheer beauty with the right musical accompaniment?

He could live with both theories, he reckoned.

And the realist in him came to the conclusion that the older you get, the lonelier you become, and the deeper the love you need.

And already, his shameless mind was busy speculating on what the soundtrack for the next woman he would meet would prove to be. Forget the hotel rooms, the railway stations where they they might first meet, or the hotel rooms that might shelter their bodies, the colour of the wallpaper, or whether she would keep her eyes open when they fuck; all he wanted to know is who she might turn out to be. He vainly tried to guess in advance what sort of song would best accompany the breathless phone tones, the unsaid longing, the sadness that would bring together their bodies.

A dance tune from Jamiroquai?

A melancholy dirge by Goldfrapp?

Jack wonders if Edwina, let alone the next unknown woman in his life, had ever listened to Grant Lee Buffalo in their glorious heyday.

33

Following the birth of their baby boy, Milduta declares to Henk that she was no longer in love with him or even in the least bit attracted to him any more. He responds by shouting at her and threatening her with violence.

She no longer cares. Now that the child is born she has automatically been granted Dutch citizenship and knows that benefits are available to her should she have to leave Henk's house for one reason or another.

She has named the boy Ivo. On the night of the birth, Henk had been out drinking with friends. For the past two months, Henk's manic depression had manifested itself in more apparent ways. His sister had warned Milduta about his moods when they had first met, after Henk had brought her to the Netherlands. But the symptoms had worsened since he had lost his job at the trade newspaper.

What is it about men, and her, she wonders. She no longer knows what she saw in him. He is like a barbarian, has no wit and all his demonstrations of affection are directly linked to his lust. Apart from money, which he has great difficulty earning, he seems to have little genuine interest in most things.

She refuses all further sexual contact with him and moves into the guest room of their canal-side house with her baby at night.

They spend whole days together under the same roof, never even talking to each other. He attempts to place some articles in magazines as there is little custom for his fledgling barge-excursions venture during the winter months, and the small trading business he has set up is slow to get off the ground properly.

He just doesn't understand her decision and the change in her attitude. She argues endlessly, pointing out he never even wanted the baby in the first place. Ivo is blond, like his father, a cherubic angel with a pleasant disposition.

To obtain some measure of independence, Milduta organises a job share with another Estonian women she has met in the same village, and they do three days a week each on the production of the local biscuit factory. The work is no challenge and the company of the other local women on the factory floor is vulgar and mindless. All they can talk about is the weather and yesterday's television programmes. On the days Milduta works, her girlfriend looks after Ivo and her own two children. The arrangement works out well for both of them and Milduta begins to save money for her planned escape from the relationship with Henk.

'Soon, I won't need you any more,' she screams at him one evening, when his attitude is more boorish than it usually is and he has forgotten to clean the baby while she was out shopping.

'You wouldn't dare leave, you cheap Russian tramp.'

'Just you see.'

'Oh, yeah? So what will you do? Find another sucker you can exploit?'

'You bastard!'

Secretly, she sees a lawyer to check what rights she has. She is determined Henk will never gain custody of Ivo, should she leave his house. She also applies to the local town hall to get her own place to live, with the child, and determines what sort of benefits she would be granted to cover the rent and the cost of for the small boy.

She hints at her likely departure when they quarrel continuously. Henk does not believe her threats and his mood grows ever resentful.

When his redundancy money has gone, and the various business prospects are not bringing in any significant cash, he is forced to take a job driving courtesy coaches between the terminals at Schipol Airport, an hour or so from their village. At least she no longer has to bear his presence on her days home.

On his first payday, he does not return home in the evening. She places his food in the microwave and goes to bed. He is home the following day and proudly tells her he went to visit a whore in the redlight district in Amsterdam the night before. Milduta just shrugs her shoulders.

'And she was much better than you. At last, a woman whose pussy gets wet and appreciates a real man's cock.'

Milduta ignores his taunts.

'No need for a description…'

'Why not?' he shouts back. 'Just because you won't have sex with me, it doesn't mean every woman is indifferent to me,' he says.

'It's only because you paid her,' Milduta laughs aloud. 'You fool…'

Henk turns scarlet and hits her on the side of her face, then manhandles her to the living-room floor, ragefully pulls her jeans open and rapes her. Milduta is still under the shock of his blow and wisely remains totally passive throughout for fear he might hit her again. She is quite dry as he wedges her thighs apart and forces himself into her with brute violence. It hurts.

While he spends himself inside her, Henk can't resist whispering further breathless threats and assorted obscenities in her ear. Milduta just closes her eyes and switches off her mind.

After he has done with her, he just stands up, his cock still half hard and dripping ejaculate, and walks silently to his bedroom to purge the alcohol still bathing his brains, leaving her spread across the floor and on the edge of tears.

She sees a doctor the next morning to get a full check-up. She is terrified he might have caught some illness with the whore and passed it on to her.

She also gives another call to the office at the town hall where she has applied for her own accommodation, and

impresses the woman bureaucrat on the other end of the line
with a renewed sense of urgency.

34

Jack stumbles almost by mistake into an Internet chat room.

His initial ventures onto the net all involved typing in the word 'sex' and gladly following where the search machines would take him. The journey was a fascinating one, widely expanding his parameters of both perversion and imagination. A sheer galaxy of pornographic web sites for every taste under the sun; alt. sex-discussion groups, interactive areas, amateur and commercial havens where absolutely anything went and more, from hirsute as well as shaven women to anal penetration, bestiality, fatties and foot fetishism, to name but a few of the more predictable kinks on open display or for sale. All this actually provided him with some good ideas for stories, as a way of justifying the increasing amount of time he was wasting in front of his computer screen and not actually working. And the sizeable telephone bills.

By force of necessity he also began to communicate by e-mail with his friends and acquaintances. It was so much more immediate and efficient, sparing him the envelopes, the stamps and the traditional walk up the road to the postbox. There was also a gently sexual frisson in communicating this way. Made letter writing so much more personal and even brought relative strangers into a risqué sphere of intimacy. Another collector, all the way away in Australia, female, wrote him a note following a piece in a magazine and very soon their correspondence took on a most personal connotation as they began to exchange the most acutely private sexual secrets and fantasies. The medium lent itself so well to this sort of flirting.

He had heard about chat rooms but had somehow never been attracted. Had always imagined it would consist of a bunch of sad people discussing, ad infinitum, the minor arcana of Star Trek or Lovecraft's Cthulhu Mythos until the sorry hours of dawn. The sort of nerds he avoided like the plague at conventions, who spelled Tolkien as Tolkein or blocked the conference hotel's stairways playing Dungeons and Dragons with a satisfied grin on their pale faces. He just knew the likely conversations in chat rooms would bore him to death or, worse, make his anger rise in a wave of exasperated irritation.

An editor in Texas had asked him for a story for a thematic anthology of all new stories about love in the third millennium. He'd agreed to pen a new tale and pencilled the delivery date in his diary, but other matters and the business of living had over-taken spring and he only remembered about the promised story with just a week to spare. He usually functioned well with close deadlines, the pressure acting as a spur for his inspiration. A sleepless night with images of countless women – past, poten-tial and somehow forgotten – cruising through his brain like a generation ship on course for distant stars, and he somehow came up with an idea. As ever, another variation on his eternal sentimental obsessions. It only took him a couple of days' work in front of his screen and, two litres of Pepsi, three bars of chocolate and much scratching of his scalp later, the story was ready: 5,200 words long. He called it 'Kiss Me Sadly'.

Off it went to Texas by DHL courier service.

He hoped it would do the trick.

Five days later, the editor of the anthology communicated back by e-mail. He loved the central idea, the characters, the final twist, thought the story had really great moments, a possi-ble prize winner. Nebula or Hugo even. But he did feel it required some changes. Not so much a rewrite, barely a few extra paragraphs, an editing job, no more.

He'd always known the stories he wrote were a bit left of field, far from ideal fodder for the popular American market, and it wasn't as if he got that many invitations to contribute to

US anthologies. There was just one editor, out there in Iowa, who was keen on his idiosyncrasies. It would be nice to widen his appeal. He replied, indicating his willingness. Maybe they should discuss the required changes over the phone? When would be the best time to call?

Forget about the phone, the answer came an hour later. I see we have the same Internet server, the editor in Texas replied. It would be both cheaper and easier to do the edit online. Fine with me, how do we do that? he asked Neil.

Easy, he was told, and was given a short set of instructions to follow on his computer screen when he logged on at the agreed time. Find 'GO' on your menu and type in 'CS3', or something of the sort.

It was a Monday, late afternoon, to cater for the time difference between north London and Austin. A series of new screen configurations waltzed across his screen. He typed in 'Yes' twice. And arrived at his chosen destination. Within seconds – he hadn't yet got his bearings or puzzled out all the boxes or sections on display – there was a 'ping', like a sort of muffled bell, and his screen opened up and there was a line there. It just said 'Neil' and 'welcome'.

He typed in 'hi' and they began the edit. Neil explained that he was recording everything his end and would then paste the changes into the story.

The whole process took only one hour and was much less extensive than he had initially feared. Neil suggested; he agreed and furnished a new line or paragraph. It would be accepted or Neil, out in Texas, would make a further suggestion. Very quickly, he grew to appreciate the ease of online editing. Another wonderful use for computers, he felt. Reminding him, ironically, how reluctant he had originally been to convert over! Felt like another life already.

There was only one drawback. At odd times during their on-screen conversation, that damn 'ping' sound would keep on going off. Pessimist that he was, he began worrying that something was wrong with his computer.

The edit was complete to their mutual satisfaction and they were just exchanging small talk when he thought to query Neil about the strange, occasional noise. Being more of a computer expert, maybe he would know what the problem might be.

'Ha ha,' Neil typed. He shouldn't worry. They were in a chat room and had forgotten to go private, so this was just other people trying to contact him. I see, he remarked, trying not to betray his inexperience.

They exchanged good-byes and Neil logged off. Back in London, he remained online and, sure enough, a few minutes later, the bell sounded again and his screen opened up to the chat box.

Dave: hi there
He replied:
106562.2021: hello
The response was fast.
Dave: where are you?
106562.2021: in London
Dave: m or f?
106562.2021: sorry?
Dave: are you male or female?
106562.2021: oh. Male.
Dave: ok. bye.

A line saying 'Dave has left the forum' appeared on the screen.

His first interlocutor disappeared. Intrigued, awaiting the next call, he moved his mouse around and began to puzzle out the possibilities on screen and soon learned he could change his subscriber number to his name. Which he did. Then clicked on the 'Who's Here' line and uncovered a long list of names, many obscene, some humorous, initials, codes, sobriquets.

The bell went off again.
9 inches: hello babe
He smiled. Answered.
How are you?
9 inches: are you dressed?

He realised that the guy at the other end assumed he was a woman.

Mischievously, he decided to play along for a while.

Jac: not totally, actually

9 inches: great… do you have big tits?

Jac: no, barely A cup I fear

9 inches: no matter, i love small boobs also. looking for fun?

Jac: why not?

Thus did Jack enter the world of chat rooms and cybersex. And role-play.

35

Milduta loved her little baby boy intensely. He was so uniquely hers, totally disassociated in her mind from Henk. She could stay there for hours, watching small Ivo gurgle, smile beatifically and purr when she caressed the velvet smoothness of his tummy. She didn't even mind his full nappies at their most odorous, or the frequent sickness so full of curdled milk and more. In a way, he made living in Henk's house still bearable. His father, on the other hand, merely looked at the new baby with curiosity. There was no unkindness present but mere puzzlement that this new, miniature human being could have issued from his seed and the Estonian girl who was giving him so much grief.

But babies also sleep much of the day, and Ivo was no exception. Actually, it even felt to Milduta that he slept more than he should, but the visiting health official reassured her this was nothing to worry about; the child ate healthily enough, although Milduta soon ran out of milk, to her great relief, as little Ivo's treatment of her nipples felt rough and painful and she was glad he moved on to powdered milk with no ill effect.

However, all this time the baby slept unfolded endlessly, leaving Milduta prey to her thoughts, stuck in the small house, watching the winter crows glide over the nearby, often frozen canal. And the longer she was alone with the questions and the doubts, the more she felt blue. And assured herself there must surely be something else, something missing from her life. Becoming a mother wasn't enough.

Henk was out most of the day, working at the airport and fiddling small jobs on the side. She taught herself to use his computer. Initially, it was just playing around, an interesting toy. Out of curiosity, she typed in the words 'sex' and 'love' into a search engine.

Within an hour she had landed in an adult chat forum and quickly got the knack of cyberflirting with the men she came across there.

It was fun.

So many men out in the whole wide world, all seeking to impress her, interested in her, talking funny or even dirty, lusting on the other side of that pulsing screen, reaching in her direction.

In her naivety, Milduta never even thought of lying to them.

Her handle was 'Mimi, Estonian Girl'.

She had no qualms about revealing who she was or her approximate geographical whereabouts (the majority of the forum members were from America, which made matters safe enough, she felt). Discovering she was in Holland elicited volleys of 'wow' and 'cool' that made her smile. Soon she was even getting invitations to visit the States, and veiled offers of free plane tickets there.

Henk had a scanner which she experimented with and, by a process of trial and error, she managed to transfer a photograph of hers onto the computer; when her suitor proved sufficiently witty or imaginative, she would even e-mail him the picture. The photo had been taken the previous summer on the deck of Henk's canal barge; Milduta smiled blissfully at the camera and her eyes looked even paler in the bright sun. She wore a brown cardigan and her hair was then cut quite short. They all loved her face and commented on the deep and pale-blue sorrow in her eyes.

'Your eyes are as deep as a sea,' one said, which stuck in her mind and she would use the expression when, in the initial online conversation, a man would, traditionally, ask her what she looked like.

Soon, they were begging her for more than just her life story and an intimate description of her body and sexual parts, and asked to speak to her over the telephone. Henk had bought her a cellphone a year or so earlier for her birthday, shortly before she had fallen pregnant and they were on relative speaking terms. She gave her number to several men and they began phoning at all hours. She had to switch the mobile phone off at night or when Ivo was sleeping in case of calls.

Some of the men introduced her to phone sex. At first she was reluctant, then reckoned it was harmless and indulged them. Most of the time she would pretend and not get naked as they requested, ignorant as they were of the Dutch winter, although on occasion, if she felt very horny, she would agree to touch herself and masturbate herself to orgasm with her eyes closed and the man's words sinking into her ear, punctuating the rise of the pleasure in her crotch.

Of course, they all went wild when they heard her accent when she spoke English. Loved it with a vengeance.

Some of the men she met on the Internet were also, she became aware, very lonely. This touched her profoundly. And many of these kept their distance, never asked for cybersex or phone sex; they just wished to talk. To these, she would explain her own sad circumstances, and elicit sympathy that momentarily warmed her soul, even though she was realistically aware that most of these men were already fantasising about the prospect of bedding this poor, Eastern-European girl in search of a better life. After all, she knew men were men. Even on the Internet.

36

The next four months witnessed a distinct downturn in Jack's work as he became badly hooked on chat-room temptations. He quickly identified the most interesting ones: Adult Entertainment, Intimate Chat Forum, Pride:BI!, NL hot Chat, France Forum. Soon, he was no longer the one always being paged and he began contacting others. Female of course. Seeking out interesting names, handles that indicated a modicum of intelligence and wit. Foreign names with a touch of enticing exoticism. But still other men kept on contacting him because of the ambiguity of his own nickname and, often, he would play along for a while, despairing at the lack of imagination they displayed. Surely he was better than them? Within a few lines, they invariably had him undressed, spread-eagled, rubbing his clit, insisting his nipples were hard and his sexual openings moist or wet depending on the season or the time of day. He did wonder what women thought of such direct, unsubtle, virtual approaches? Obviously, some would go along with the fantasies just for the fun of it, but he couldn't believe that's what women wanted.

In his own approaches, he was careful not to move onto sexual matters until well into the conversation. He was more interested in them as persons, the voyeur in him fascinated to learn about their life, the reasons that brought them onto the forums. Some momentarily even became friends before suddenly disappearing, with no word of warning, from the virtual world (or, more likely, moving on to chat rooms with another server). He loved it. This was a wonderful way of meeting others. So easy and straightforward. He'd never been the sort of person to walk up to others in bars or at parties, and had always been too shy to begin a conversation with an attractive woman in a bus queue or sitting across from him in an underground carriage. But this was so easy. There were no barriers, no opportunities for embarrassment. Rejection, if rejection there was, was impersonal and painless.

There was the opera singer in New York. The banker in Toronto who called herself Montana and called him the sunshine of her life and sent him a couple of nude photographs of herself. She was married with two kids but had a wonderful figure. He came across a dark-haired Gypsy woman from Aix-en-Provence in the south of France, who sent him a fully clothed photo and suggested they meet for real. After toying with the idea, he agreed and took a plane and spent a weekend there with her in a narrow hotel room. The photo had been taken ten years before, and instead of the single child she had admitted to, he discovered she actually had four, but no husband. The sex was good but they found they had little to say to each other and seldom spoke online again after they both returned to their computers. All he remembered of her later was the sublime vision of her perfectly shaped arse as she walked away from the bed to the bathroom on the first morning.

Then there was the student in south Carolina who collected photographs of men with large endowments and made it clear she wouldn't sleep with him but still enjoyed discussing the aesthetics of cocks, and the pros and cons of cut vs uncut penises and shaved vs unshaven balls. He knew that she did meet several men through the chat room during the time of their contact – she had a substantial trust fund and was free to travel places for the right fuck – as she lovingly provided him with all the anatomical details of her couplings. The college year ended and she never reappeared on the forum. There was another student in Berkshire, closer to home, who was torn between her urge to lose her cumbersome virginity and her attraction to female classmates. Her name was Jenni and she also e-mailed him a photo she had taken of herself and scanned. Skinny as hell, with adorable small breasts and green thong panties, and awkwardly posing for the Polaroid in her study. When the picture provoked a hard-on, he felt like a paedophile; she couldn't be more than fifteen.

And then there was Rachel.

He couldn't recall their first chat. Who had called whom first. By now, he no longer logged on as '106562,2021' but as 'Londonwriter (m)', having grown tired of all the unimaginative chat-up lines conjured up by other men.

She was American, lived in Paris, where she worked for some financial consultancy organisation. She was in her late twenties, and had a daughter who was six years old. Rebecca. Her divorce was in the last throes of paperwork. From the first few conversations onwards, Jack took a strong liking to her. Her voice on screen seemed real, pleasant, quietly vulnerable.

Rachel came from a Wasp background and had been to the French Lycée in New York, before moving on to an Ivy League university. Not only did she live in France but, after a few weeks, he discovered much his pleasant surprise that she knew and enjoyed French culture as much as he did. Discussing films or books, she had the most amazing knowledge of peculiarly obscure writers or movies.

She had married young, a much older University lecturer who had been a family friend. Almost twenty years her senior. Someone she could look up to, maybe a father figure of sorts; hers had died when she was still young. The first years of the marriage had been happy despite the difference in their ages, but following the birth of Rebecca, on whom they both doted, they began inexorably to grow apart. He became increasingly jealous, abusive even, and eventually Rachel felt she had no alternative but to separate. The company she worked for on Wall Street had agreed to transfer her to the Paris office and she had now been in the French capital over six months, while the legal formalities were completed. Every two months, Rebecca would spend a couple of weeks with her father, who had not accepted the separation lightly and was seeking to gain custody of her. But Rachel's lawyers were confident he would not succeed in this.

At no stage in their early chats did Rachel even hint at sexual elements and their conversation soon adapted to a comfortable groove of life stories, discussion of books, films and music, and a gentle flirting where much was left unsaid.

He expressed his curiosity for what she looked like. She had, in a perennial piece of Internet etiquette, provided her description and statistics earlier and the mental image Jack had fabricated of her was already well on the way to quiet perfection. Tall, blonde, gently spoken. She volunteered to send him a photograph by e-mail.

When it arrived, he opened the jpg with a nervous butterfly coursing around his stomach. But the results were enchanting. She was beautiful. Very American; long-haired; pretty in an understated woman-next-door way; pale skinned, dark, sad eyes scoring a bull's-eye on his heart.

Every day, they would meet online in the forum around three o'clock and talk for at least an hour. Sometimes they were interrupted – after all, she had a job to do – and sometimes her answers were slow in coming and he assumed that she was also talking to others.

There were days when she was melancholy and he could feel her unhappiness invade the bright page on the screen. Loneliness, difficulties with the legal process, the child's minor illnesses, homesickness. Other days, Rachel turned playful, teasing him mercilessly on his insistence to forego cybersex with her, describing her clothes in minute details, how her office was overheated and she had taken off her pantyhose or opened her shirt, letting him imagine the delights thus uncovered. Or she would hide from him in the list of online names, assuming pseudonyms from books or movies which he would invariably and proudly recognise, however difficult she made the task. He would do likewise but he knew she had the latest server software and could identify him much more easily if she had clicked on his number under 'friends' and saved it; a function he did not possess.

So, following on from a light-hearted discussion about James Joyce, she would masquerade as 'Nora' or 'Anna Livia Plurabelle' or 'Dublin gal', or on another occasion adopt the persona of most of the female protagonists of *Gone with the Wind*. Once, he wasn't sure how their talk had moved on to Nabokov, she had hidden amongst the list as 'Dolores Haze', 'Butterfly' or 'Lepidoptera'. No easy 'Lolita' for Rachel!

He could only smile, ravished as he was by the elegance of her repartee and imagination.

She even gave him her mobile telephone number.

He readily agreed he would never phone her unless they agreed a time to do so beforehand.

Her voice did not disappoint.

Breathy, moving from childish to pleading to joyful in the breadth of a few sentences; talking about her day, her love for her child, her apprehensions about what her erstwhile husband was up to. They tried to speak at least once a week. His heart moved with the ups and downs of Rachel's fleeting moods.

The lines on screen, the photograph saved away in his documents file, the voice. Jack was hooked.

Badly.

She knew he wrote but had never expressed much curiosity for his stories. On a few occasions, he volunteered to post her some copies but she always asked him to wait. 'Later' she would say, as if she wanted to make the pleasure last somehow.

On the phone. One day.

'I'm falling for you,' he said.

'Are you?' she answered, expressionless.

'I am, Rachel.'

'I like you too,' she said.

For the first time, the possibility of the two of them actually meeting in real life reared its head. After all, London and Paris were barely three hours apart with the Eurostar train.

He was slow to suggest it. After all, the possibility of being disappointed by her was something he was scared of. Was the photo he had actually of her? Was it genuinely taken the previous year (unlike Mireille's)? But once he searched himself, he knew that the voice on the phone corresponded so beautifully with the face on his screen. Quiet, sad, melancholy, vulnerable. All the things that attracted him in Rachel, beyond her innate culture and intelligence and the fact that conversing her was such an easy delight.

At first, he felt all he should propose was to meet her after her day at the office and have a drink, a coffee together, maybe even a meal.

'I would like that, Jack,' she answered.

'I must come to Paris soon to see my French publishers,' he added. 'I will let you know as soon as I have a precise date for the trip.' He had no wish to reveal how much she now meant to him and the fact he was quite willing to go to Paris just to see her.

'Great.'

That weekend, he wrote her a long letter, tactfully alluding to his feelings, carefully hinting that he held her in much respect and wasn't expecting sex or an affair automatically, confessing to his previous Internet-inspired jaunt to France for the weekend with Mireille. He wanted her to know he did not think of her in the same way, that his feelings were both strong and genuine, even though the way they had met was so uncommon, nay bizarre. He polished his words endlessly over two days, putting in more rewrites to the letter to Rachel than he had done on any of his recent novels. He e-mailed it to her.

She did not respond to it and no mention was made of the letter in their online chats later in the week. Maybe he had gone too far, he wondered. Or maybe Rachel was exquisitely discreet and wished to spare his feelings.

But she did ask again when he would come to Paris.

37

Was it her photograph or her words, her voice or the sorrow of her situation, living with a man she could no longer love – but had she ever? – that attracted the men from the Internet to Milduta? Like flies. Like bees to honey.

The more they discovered of her, the keener they became to actually meet her.

At first, she shied away from the idea, but thoughts of maybe this and then maybe that began to undermine her caution and she would speculate wildly about the personalities behind the voices and the seductive phrases on her computer screen. Or the eyes full of alternatively kindness or desire. Or the bodies. The reality of these strangers.

Although her written English was halting and riddled with mistakes, she enjoyed the cybersex in all its arcane and arousing, if theoretical, extremities. It made her head burn and sometimes her imagination would take flight from a suggested situation and conjure further delights well beyond the reach of the words parading on her screen, and her loins would tingle and her heart beat faster. Momentarily feed her hunger.

She began to grade her virtual suitors by the variations they offered in the often repetitive cyber-embraces and sundry penetrations and variety of sexual positions they would propose for their mutual fornication.

Milduta had never before guessed how much the power of words could affect her feverish imagination. Maybe it was because she was stuck in the Dutch countryside with a baby, away from worldly temptations and her bad habits and compulsions of old. She was even shocked at how often she would become wet, sitting there at her keyboard – sometimes with Ivo actually dozing in her lap – while her mind raced from situation to situation, imagining what the sex that one stranger or another suggested might be like in real life.

The men lying patiently in wait on the other side of her flat computer screen ran merrily through the whole encyclopaedia of human sexual practices, volumes full, as they chatted on-screen or over the telephone when she was able to pick up their calls on her cellphone, when Henk was not around, as they mostly called in the evening. They were in turn perverse, disgusting, shocking, utterly surprising, tempting, breakers of every taboo imaginable, exploiters, madmen, masters of the bedroom, fuckers for all seasons and more.

She met a banker who lived in Zurich, Switzerland.

She would usually share herself between three or four conversations when online. Flit between them on her screen. It was unusual for one man alone to keep her attention long enough until her mind wandered as he ran out of questions or dialogue beyond the opening interrogation and typical enquiries about her gender, her state of clothing or unclothing, her vital statistics, whether she was hot or in search of fun.

The banker straight away seemed more interesting. More decisive.

Ten to fifteen short lines into their conversation, he had asked whether she was speaking to any others.

She had confirmed this and he had immediately ordered her to abandon the other conversations and speak exclusively to him.

Milduta had agreed and closed the other windows.

His name was Max.

For six weeks, they arranged to meet online between 3pm and 4pm every afternoon. Weekends proved more difficult because of Henk's likely presence and use of the computer. She was allowed to speak to others during the rest of the day or evening, should she wish. Milduta and Max missed very few of the agreed appointments.

He was imaginative. And different from the men she had come across before, whether in real life or during the course of her tentative online activities.

He could also make her laugh.

Neither Serge nor Henk had never managed that minor feat. And she recalled how her grandparents used to say how beautiful she was when she laughed. It felt like a long time ago.

They exchanged photos.

He didn't look anything special, but she knew by now that appearances could be deceptive and she had not been a particularly accurate judge of character in her life so far when it came to men.

He looked just like a bank manager, which came as no surprise; severe glasses, a receding hairline, a dark suit, immaculately pressed white shirt with starched collar and grey tie. There was also a hint of cruelty in his eyes which both chilled her and strangely beckoned her towards him.

Max said he wanted to meet her and would come to Amsterdam.

She lied to Henk that she was meeting a girlfriend from Estonia who was passing through the city and that, not to rush their reunion, she had agreed to stay with her overnight. He reluctantly agreed to look after Ivo, after Milduta rehearsed him in nappy changing and prepared the child's food so that he would only have to reheat it.

Max was punctual as she had expected and was on the platform where her local train alighted that early evening at the Amsterdam Centraal Station. He saw her disembark from the carriage and allowed himself a thin smile. He greeted her with sobriety and kissed her hand. Milduta was nervous, having already committed herself not to return to Henk's house tonight. If anything were to go wrong, she would have to roam the streets of Amsterdam or the railway station until the first available train back in the morning.

They had coffees at a bar outside the station, merely exchanging small talk.

Max then led her to a visibly expensive French restaurant just off Prinsengracht, where he had a booking. Milduta felt slightly out of place. She wore her black suit and a simple white blouse, probably her best outfit but much too simple and inelegant for this sort of place.

After they had ordered from the elaborate menu, Max handed her a small box and bid her open it.

It contained a thin, gold ankle chain.

'I want you to get up now, walk to the ladies' washroom and put it on, Mimi,' he said calmly. 'When you return, you will be wearing my chain, as witness to the fact that, until tomorrow morning, you belong to me.'

Milduta lowered her eyes, at a loss for words.

The chain must have cost a lot, she knew.

She rose.

After dinner, they walked to the Krasnapolsky Hotel, off the Dam, where he had booked into.

Following Max through the lobby, Milduta felt like a whore who had just sold herself. And found the thought particularly arousing.

In the room, Max fucked her three times during the course of a mostly sleepless night, exploring her body with systematic attention. On each occasion, he insisted on mounting her doggie style.

38

Jack and Rachel were chatting online late one afternoon when he suggested he could take a midday train the following weekend. She greeted the news calmly. He told her he would make a Eurostar booking and arrange a hotel and would confirm by e-mail a few hours later.

There is no need to stay in a hotel and spend money unnecessarily, she said on screen. You can stay at my place.

Are you sure? he queried, though his heart and loins danced a light fandango.

Of course, she answered. There is a spare bedroom anyway, if we don't get on.

The hint was of course present that the spare bedroom wouldn't prove necessary.

Rebecca's father would be in Europe that week and he would be taking care of her. It was his turn.

He breathed deeply. All the right elements were in place.

He logged off after some more small talk and quickly made his train reservation.

The following day, he confirmed his arrangements with her and, always cautious, just in case the train arrived late and he was unable to meet up with her at the cafe on the Champs Elysées, close to her office, as arranged, he asked her for her home address. She lived on the Avenue Victor Hugo, a stone's throw from the Arc de Triomphe. He noted the number.

Their next conversations saw him walking on air in expectation of Paris. It was all falling into place, too good to be true. They spoke once more on the phone and again he was enchanted by the sheer tone of her voice. He knew he was in love. Even though he'd not yet actually met her; it was illogical, crazy and wonderful. And, deep inside, he was convinced she would not disappoint, would be even better in real life. Looked forward to the moving shades of darkness of her eyes; the small blemishes on her skin; the pale hue of her uncovered shoulders; the fragrant smell of her breath; the warmth radiating outwards from her body as they sat together at a restaurant table discussing Julien Green or André Pieyre de Mandiargues, both authors they had discovered a common liking for.

He had informed some French book dealers he would be in town; some tax-exemption documents from a previous deal had to be signed and a look at their new stock would save waiting for their next catalogues.

Two days before his trip, the main dealer rang with the news of a family ailment and asked could he postpone his trip by six days.

He reluctantly agreed and informed Rachel. She didn't appear too distraught by the change of plan and reminded him that she would not be in Paris the following week, as she had a business trip to Rome already set up. He did recall her mentioning this some time back. It was agreed he would come to Paris again for her a fortnight later. There was no rush anyway, was there? Of course not, he acquiesced. After all, Rachel would always be there. Barely three hours away from him by train. The thought warmed him. The conversation moved to what she was wearing today and she teased him again insufferably, lingering insistently on the fabric of her brassiere and how flushed she could get now that summer was nearing.

By the end of their online chat, he had a respectable hard-on.

The dealer's new stock was a disappointment.

Jack had an afternoon to spare before the Eurostar back to London after his publisher had lunched him. There was an alternate country CD he knew had been released early in France as the band was touring there, so he took a trip to the

Virgin Megastore next to the Lido on the Champs Elysées to purchase it. He exited the store with a further four records; he'd always been a bad, voracious shopper when it came to music. The weather was turning grey and he pondered catching a movie. Which is when he noticed the flower stall and decided to get flowers for Rachel. Act with a modicum of elegance. He knew she was still in Rome, wouldn't be back for another two days, but surely it would be a nice surprise to find a lovely bouquet on her doorstep as she returned. He carefully supervised the selection of colourful flowers until the bunch looked eminently spectacular and called a cab. The block of flats on the Avenue Victor Hugo looked prosperous. The intercom only displayed the flat numbers and he realised he didn't know in which one Rachel lived. He rang for the concierge and the heavy, wooden front door clicked open. He made his way down the darkened corridor until he found the window to the concierge's ground-floor apartment. Knocked. The woman looked at him wearily; maybe she thought he was a delivery person for the flowers. He asked for Rachel. She appeared puzzled. He repeated his request, describing her, a young American woman with a small daughter; Rachel McKenna. The concierge mumbled negatively. Maybe she was known here under her married name. He inquired: Rachel Stewart? No again. The concierge was adamant, there was no American in the whole block, he must be mistaken. He abandoned the flowers in a wheelie-bin on the Avenue as he walked back towards the Rond-Point to catch a cab. Evidently, she had furnished him with a wrong address. Why? He couldn't fathom the answer. His heart now felt heavy. He brooded all the way back to London, in search of an answer. In vain. Rachel had lied to him.

As he emerged from the Waterloo terminal, the heavens opened and the rain bucketed down as if it were Judgement Day.

39

The soundtrack floats upwards once again.

Muted rumblings from the brass section emerge towards the slow back beat of the normally plaintive melody, interrupting its smooth, sad flow. Then the pace of the song, of the music, quickens imperceptibly to the human ear.

40

A few days passed as he buckled down to his usual routine, hesitant to log on again to the forum while the unpleasant scar of Rachel's lies festered inside him.

Finally, he could resist no longer.

Half an hour online later, having ignored several 'm or f'? requests, he saw her handle appear in the 'who's here' column. Rachel.

He paged her.

Londonwriter (m): hi

It took her a long time to respond, as if she was already immersed in a variety of conversations with other forum members.

Rachel: hi

Londonwriter (m): how was Rome?

Rachel: ok, a bit boring

Londonwriter (m): some good meals at least?

Rachel: oh yes. You should see me in the bathroom mirror when I come out of the shower. I've put weight on. I'm gross...

Londonwriter (m): i'm sure that a few meals won't have made such a difference. Even fat, I'll have you readily.... (s)

Rachel: nice of you to say so. So.... how did the interview go?

Londonwriter (m): predictable

Rachel: oh

He hesitated a minute or two, waiting for her to relaunch the conversation, but she didn't. So he took the plunge.

Londonwriter (m): you know...

Rachel: yes?

Londonwriter (m): while I was in Paris last week, I thought I'd buy you some flowers….

Rachel: that's nice

Londonwriter (m): but they hadn't heard of you, Avenue Victor Hugo… why did you give me a wrong address, Rachel?

Rachel: oh, that…

She fell silent.

Londonwriter (m): I understand that one has to be so careful with Internet encounters, but surely you knew you could trust me.

…………………

Londonwriter (m): anyway, it doesn't matter, Rachel. It really doesn't…

…………………

Londonwriter (m): Rachel?

…………………

Londonwriter (m): talk to me, please

(Rachel has left the forum)

For the rest of the week, she didn't come onto the forum. Finally, he called her up. She picked up, said 'hello'. 'It's me,' he said, 'can we talk?' She hung up. He knew he had broken one of the rules not to call her on the telephone unless previously agreed. Maybe she had been in a meeting. He gave it a few more days.

He sent her an e-mail, telling her it was all right, he forgave her, but still wanted to be friends, stay in touch.

She didn't answer.

A second e-mail, which he had configured so that he would be informed when she picked it up, remained unopened in her box.

He rang her once more. By now, his thoughts were frantic, the Rachel scenarios racing through his brain, taking over his life, causing him to miss work deadlines because of the profound upset. This time, her mobile number was no longer functioning and all he got was a message in French informing her that the number had been discontinued.

One more e-mail.

It bounced back to him. She had closed her server account.

Rachel had disappeared from the Internet and his life altogether.

For weeks, he mourned quietly as he began to pick up the pieces of his life again. But he just couldn't understand. Why? Why? Why?

The sorrow turned to anger and he carefully composed a message which he posted on the bulletin board of the forum.

HAS ANYONE HERE RECENTLY BEEN IN TOUCH WITH RACHEL STEWART MCKENNA? IF YOU HAVE, CONTACT ME ON 106562.2021. DISCRETION ASSURED.

He doubted there would be any comeback. As it was, he seldom even looked up the messages there himself, restricting himself to the chat rooms as did the majority of users and visitors who were content with hot chat or anonymous flirting.

He had to leave London for a few days and didn't take his laptop along.

When he returned, there were six messages in response to his enquiry.

All from other men who had been in regular contact with the elusive Rachel.

He began corresponding with all of them.

The sky fell.

For CK in Milton Keynes, she had been a banking executive based in Brussels. Single and without child. For months already, they had been having torrid cybersex, the best he had ever had, on a daily basis and had been planning to meet in Los Angeles a few weeks hence for a dirty weekend which had been planned in the minutest sexual detail. Thinking how reserved Rachel and he had been online, Jack blushed and cursed CK silently. She had cuckolded him. Virtually, at any rate.

For D (m-NYC), Rachel was an attorney in Boston. Childless, divorced, lonely. They had also been scheduled to meet up in real life very soon. He was reluctant to furnish more details about their online relationship.

For Lestat, she had been a bartender in Omaha. And a very hot chick.

For Ian, real-life location unknown, she had also been living in Paris but was a student and a nymphomaniac who enjoyed providing exhilarating details of her casual fucks with the men she would pick up in the Latin Quarter cafes, and hinted at a future threesome if he could make the journey there.

For Michael in San Diego, she was an actress living in New York who could only get her kicks from anal sex and loved to reminisce about cocks she had known and been invaded by.

For Responsive (Paris), she had actually been in London, a lecturer at the local French Lycée in Kensington and was planning a visit to him by Eurostar soonest, with delightful hints of common pleasures on the occasion.

And all the while, for Jack, she had just been Rachel; demure, pretty, quietly unhappy.

If six men had answered his call, he reckoned there must be at least as many others who hadn't even come across his message! It seemed Rachel, a great actress in the making, had juggled them all with dexterity and wit.

And disappeared from the forum at the same time, promises unfulfilled, bathed in mystery and possibilities.

They all missed her in different ways.

They had all been sent her photo and been captivated by her. It sounded as if it was the same photo, but Jack couldn't be certain. Vulnerable soul, whore, teaser, splendid creature, somehow conjured by their imaginations and personal obsessions. She had been all things to all men and briefly made some happy by providing hope of sex, friendship, lust and even love.

Jack was no longer angry at her. At least it appeared he was the only man she had given her telephone number too and actually spoken to. And he knew, from the dialling code, that she was genuinely living in Paris. So maybe his version of Rachel was the real one. And all the others were playful, ersatz versions of her; cruder, ruder.

He couldn't stop admiring the girl.

Sitting there at her keyboard, surfing forums with gay abandon (who was to say she didn't also roam other forums on other servers, up to her confounding tricks?), pulling the pitiful strings of men all over like a master puppeteer.

Jack? Oh yes, London, middle-aged, falling in love with me. Thinks I'm a single mother going through a difficult divorce.

CK? British businessman who likes it dirty, scenarios full of bondage and rough sex. Believes I'm single, unattached and always willing.

Lestat? Likes me to talk filthy and pretend I'm masturbating. Omaha barmaid, with big sexual history.

And on and on.

Maybe she even had a little black notebook, with all of them carefully filed away, with their tastes and idiosyncrasies. If it's Monday, it must be Jack; be shy. If it's Tuesday, it must be Michael; be outrageous.

She juggled with their lives and feelings with the talent of a magician, knew what made them tick, watched them dance before her playful eyes; but did she find the circus pleasurable, Jack wondered? Why did she do it? Was it really only a game?

He had no answers and wondered daily what had happened to her. Did she retire or was she playing the same old games on some other forum, in some distant chat room he knew nothing of?

She was good, he had to concede that. Give the gal an Oscar.

41

Jack and Milduta met online.

He was now 'melancholy' and she was still 'Estonian Girl'.

He was the one to page her, mildly intrigued by her exotic provenance and possibilities. Maybe assuming she was blonde.

Following the halting introductions and uneasy expressions of interest, he politely declined her offer for them to have cybersex.

'It's just words, you see. Does nothing for me.'

'I know, but sometime you not do real, is good anyway,' she answered.

'Sorry, just not my scene,' he typed. 'But I would like to chat to you more. I'm sure there are a lot of things we can talk about.'

Their lines of text bounced to and fro, across cyberspace and countries.

His curiosity was piqued.

She told him her story.

How she had followed this Belgian student to the West, abandoned him for his Dutch acquaintance and ended up in a small house by a canal in Northern Holland, out of love and now mother to a lovely baby boy. How she found life boring and was hoping for something more.

He revealed his reasons for being in this chat room.

Told her about how he had met Edwina and how they had fallen into this wonderful, intense affair and of the shock of rejection and the way its aftermath still affected him, even such a long time later.

They fell into a comfortable routine of speaking daily on-screen, although there were also frequent times when Milduta would ignore him on the occasions Jack paged her.

No doubt, he guessed, she was too busy right then indulging in virtual sex with other forum members to steal herself away for his milder words and preoccupations. He was amused by her and this carefree attitude she openly displayed of releasing her sexual frustrations and indulging herself with the harmless fantasies of other guys. In fact, she would willingly provide him with fascinating tidbits and detailed descriptions of some of the quirks she encountered and even enjoyed. Jack admired her and looked forward to her tales of Internet adventure, never for a moment feeling the slightest twinge of jealousy. How could you begrudge such a free spirit her small joys?

Their dialogue continued in fits and starts over a whole month.

But Jack, still cautious following the abortive encounter with Rachel, felt in no rush to force the pace. He had no desire to run before he could metaphorically walk with Milduta.

She was quietly intrigued by his apparent reticence. Unlike so many of the other men she spoke to, he was not making any wild and rash promise of coming to meet her in Holland, or suggesting slyly he might pay for her to come to him.

She sent him the photo taken on Henk's barge. So full of her beaming smile.

He acknowledged her prettiness.

Then, later, another photo, more serious and sober, of her sitting at a table in the castle at Nijmegen, in her black suit, her hands crossed, looking ever so grown-up and sad. As she expected, he much preferred that particular photograph, her curious Mr Melancholy of London!

The day following her tryst at the Krasnapolsky Hotel with Max, she excitedly revealed to Jack that the man from Zurich (she had actually hinted she might be meeting him in real life in a previous online chat but Jack hadn't attached too much importance to the boast) wanted her to come and live with him in Switzerland, and had agreed she could bring the child, Ivo, with her.

Jack was surprised.

Began to regret his caution and slowness. Why could he never dictate the pace of relationships, he blamed himself?

'Will you go?' he asked Milduta.

She explained how, when she had returned home from Amsterdam the next morning, Henk had just taken a look at her face and exploded. Just from the shine in her eyes, he had revealed, he just knew that she had been getting her brains fucked out all night. Milduta had sighed wearily, knowing that she just couldn't conceal some things. Of course, she had denied it, but it hadn't done much good. He visibly didn't believe her and had stormed out to go to his work at the airport. Neither had he bothered to change Ivo's nappies one single time while Milduta had been away; the baby had a terrible rash all over his tender backside and his bed was just soaked.

Before Henk's terrible anger, Milduta had been in two minds about Max's proposal. There was something about the Swiss banker she was still a trifle nervous about. Couldn't put her finger on it precisely, although she knew that her inner core responded guiltily to his assertiveness and demands.

Henk's attitude had, in a way, forced the decision on her.

She would travel to Zurich.

Jack was the first she was confiding in. What did he think?

'I just don't know,' he typed. 'Not for me to advise. Any suggestion I would make would be utterly prejudiced, you see.'

'You always use difficult words,' Milduta replied, 'but I know what you try say, Jack.'

'Do you?'

'Yes, Jack, but Max, he make offer and you never do…'

'I know.'

'We try keep touch, no?'

'We try. And…'

'What, Jack?'

'Good luck, Milduta. I mean it.'

'You are nice man, Jack. I not forget you.'

'You'd better not,' he smiled as he logged off, already nostalgic for the Estonian girl.

After all, maybe it was a genuine chance for her to start all over again. New country, new man, financial security. How could he begrudge her that?

Impulsively he moved back to the forum, seeking her handle on the lengthy list. She was no longer online.

He nodded, scanning the lines scrolling up and down his computer screen until his eyes lost focus and all the words and names were out of reach.

He wondered absent-mindedly whether they would remain in contact any longer. Chat again. Probably not. Her Swiss guy was unlikely to encourage her playing online now.

Jack filed her two photographs away in an old folder, convinced this would be the last he would ever hear of Milduta.

And he still had so many questions he had forgotten to ask her.

42

When she informs Henk that evening that she is leaving him and is planning to go live with another man, in Zurich of all places, he is absolutely furious. She does not wear the ankle chain she has been given by Max and keeps it concealed at the bottom of her handbag.

He makes dire threats and expressly forbids her to take their child along. Milduta and he argue endlessly every evening that week. She has already checked with a local Citizens Advice Bureau about her legal rights as the child's mother and knows she can take Ivo with her, as long as she does not state that her absence from the Netherlands is to be permanent. She bides her time, awaiting the rail tickets and other arrangements Max is making right now.

The night before she is supposed to leave for Switzerland, although he is unaware of the fact her preparations are so advanced, she and Henk come to blows as the conversation grows increasingly heated. He smacks her on the face, and draws a thin sliver of blood from the small cut across her cheekbone. She kicks him several times. Ivo, woken and suffering from toothache, is left to bawl for over an hour as Milduta and Henk tear each other apart, all the resentment and anger surfacing with astonishing bile and violence.

The next day is a Saturday and he isn't working.

She uses the bruise on her face as a necessary excuse and Henk is left to do the food shopping. The supermarket is a couple of kilometres away in the closest town. The moment he drives off, Milduta calls for a taxi and packs hurriedly, stuffing as much of her clothes and Ivo's as possible into the only two suitcases she can find in the house. She is forced to leave much behind.

The cab mercifully arrives for her before Henk returns from his shopping, and delivers Milduta and Ivo at Amsterdam's Centraal Station. The connection to Zurich is in Frankfurt.

Max's apartment in the Swiss city is a delight. All modern furnishings and sleek fixtures and spare, clean lines, immaculately laid out and shiny clean. Such a contrast with Henk's untidy and cluttered house, where she always had to fight a losing battle with the advancing dust. Milduta immediately feels she has taken the right decision to come here. Max had cleared a small room he used as a study for the baby, and had it redecorated in cheerful wallpaper and installed a cot there. Milduta realised this was the first time she would not be sleeping in the same room as her child. It somehow hadn't occurred to her until now that Max was unlikely to want to have Ivo in the same bedroom where he would also fuck her.

He takes her shopping and purchases new clothes for her. He is the one who selects the items; seldom asks for her opinion. He has definite views as to how she should dress. Short skirts are the order of the day, and stockings. The underwear he selects is both expensive and daring. He has her throw much of her previous undergarments away; finds them too dowdy.

She settles into life with the banker. Although he is generous with his gifts and the things he buys her, he does not provide her with money, and she is forced to save a little, franc by franc, from what he gives her to get food while he is away working. During the days, she wanders the streets of the harsh new city she is living in, still amazed by the abundance of goods and its gloomy lack of personality. Milduta does not understand German and finds communication with shopkeepers difficult.

She tries to use Max's home laptop computer, but there is a password preventing her access which she cannot crack.

At night, once Ivo is safely asleep and tucked comfortably into his small bedroom, Max's sexual attentions and imperious demands overwhelm her, but she can't help but enjoy the state of submission he imposes on her; the dovetailing to his orders and sometimes humiliating postures he has her adopt or the total lack of privacy he imposes on her when they are together, even when she has need to go to the toilet; the games of slavery he has her play. It arouses her more than she thought.

'You suck cock like a high-class whore,' he remarks.

She takes pride in his compliment.

Quickly, the Swiss man's demands become more extreme.

He explains the gospel of bdsm to her. The compact between Master and submissive. How she must also take pleasure from the love she grants her dominant Master. Psychological as well as physical pleasure are to be seen as equal as they explore her limits. She is not quite certain she understands it all, but does respond to certain elements she earlier would have found utterly shameful. He wishes to train her. She is to become his submissive. His slave, almost.

It is no longer to be just a game.

Even though Milduta recognises the foundations of submission within her, her mind nonetheless rebels. Total dependence just goes against her nature.

Max orders her to keep her sexual parts shaven at all times, although she finds it sometimes brings the sensitive skin around her pussy out in a rash. He purchases leather harnesses and enjoys taking photographs of Milduta in their embrace and obligatory revealing positions. One image he takes a strong liking to and has the print blown up to almost life-size proportions and has it hanging above their bed. Milduta protests that the cleaning woman would see it.

'So what?' Max responds.

And every time he fucks her while she squats on all fours, her eyes are drawn again and again to the shocking photograph on the wall facing her of her wide-open cunt, spread apart by a black leather dildo buried deep within her meaty folds. At least, she consoled herself with the fact that only they and the cleaner ever entered this room, and she studiously avoided the dour woman on her weekly visit to look after the apartment, always arranging to take Ivo for a walk in his buggy.

One day, he demands she wear the thin dog collar he has acquired and pronounces he will take her to private parties as his slave, and should he so feel inclined, allow her to be used by other men in his presence, to share her. Declares that her cocksucking talent should be demonstrated to the world at large.

Milduta stays silent as her heart drops.

He becomes increasingly angry with her whenever she has left a cushion or a magazine out of position or unwittingly disturbed the decorative harmony of the apartment and left the slightest thing untidy. Regardless of his sexual world view, she finds Max awfully petty now.

On a Thursday night, having spent a full hour that evening training her in the art of the right posture and displaying her assets while partly shackled and immobilised by a metal spread bar attached to her ankles – which she finally got right after a series of punitive spankings – Max announced proudly, as he stroked her cheek with proprietorial affection, that Milduta was now ready to be introduced to the right circles. Her mind raced ahead, infected by a sense of panic.

The next morning she left Zurich in haste, counting out just enough francs to get the off-peak train tickets.

She landed back on Henk's doorstep only three-and-a-half weeks after her initial flight.

She had nowhere else to go.

It was either Henk or Tallinn.

43

By now, Jack could no longer deny that he was suffering from a bad case of Internet addiction.

There were so many souls, women out there, beautiful strangers, hanging in fragile equilibrium in what William Gibson had once baptised cyberspace, both within reach and also tantalisingly out of reach, so full of promises and untold delights, and it was difficult for him to stay away, even if he knew that only one out of a hundred contacts might pan out into something more significant. He even doubted he had the patience or energy any longer to follow-through again on the road to some new, problematic relationship, with all its obstacles and likely problems.

Still, he returned to his screen and explored.

So many in the chat rooms, beyond the frequently ridiculous or boastful pseudonyms they often chose to adopt or their veiled advertising for out-of-the-way if not illegal sex, professed to be bisexual. Jack had seldom given the matter any thought.

Most times it was a case of women seeking women.

On one occasion, a man contacted him and, on discovering he was actually male – 'melancholy' led many interlocutors to believe he was, in fact, female – seriously inquired, as he realised they were both in the same city, whether Jack might be interested in an encounter.

Indicating that he was not gay, Jack was surprised to see the unknown man respond, saying 'neither am I'.

melancholy: so why are you making me an offer?

Valiant: I swing both ways. I like women, you see, but actually cock is also nice.

melancholy: really?

Valiant: You should try it. You might be well surprised.

melancholy: I somehow doubt it. In fact, I'm sadly confident the sight of another man's penis wouldn't even get me hard. I'm just not attracted, basically. It's just not like a woman's body, doesn't strike the same chords at all.

Valiant: Never even thought of it? Be honest.

Jack pondered a short while.

He understood women together; there was a beauty, an aesthetic attraction to a woman's nudity. Maybe if he had been born female, he would have been bisexual, wanted the best of both worlds. But men?

melancholy: I just don't feel drawn to the idea of fucking a man in the anus, or being fucked myself. That's the bottom line. I have never been physically attracted to a man. No way. No prejudice, you understand.

Valiant: That's not what I meant. What about fellatio? Think about it. Has it never occurred to you to wonder what it feels for a woman to take a cock in her mouth? What it tastes like? What the sensation of sucking cock must be? To be on the other side, so to speak.

Jack had, he agreed.

So many women had, naturally, given him head over the years and he had intermittently speculated on what sort of pleasure it afforded them, or whether it was just some sexual act they were resigned to because of tradition or force of habit, guessing it would mollify their partner. The act felt so much like a one-way exchange of power.

The conversation petered out but his mind kept on returning to it over the following weeks.

All of a sudden, every time he logged on to the Internet, everyone appeared to be bisexual and he was in a distinct minority.

As his imagination continued its instinctive journey over these risky waters, Jack became consumed with a terrible curiosity, even though the whole idea radically went against everything he knew of himself and his sexual inclinations.

But the idea had taken root, however much he tried to resist it and all the necessary implications.

A blue day came when the loneliness just became too much and Jack entered into another dialogue. The man held court as 'nicholas m for m'.

He was on the other side of town, at the end of Jack's underground line.

One hour later, he was sitting on a ramshackle bedsit's couch in Leytonstone, naked, with the other man giving him a blow job. He had warned him it was to be his first time and that he was worried he would not even achieve a proper erection. The moment the stranger's mouth wrapped itself around his cock, he grew hard without fail.

Jack had closed his eyes but there was no point in pretending it was a woman giving him a blow job, although it felt just the same. A mouth was a mouth.

'Want to try, mate?' the other man had suggested after sucking Jack off.

'OK,' Jack replied nervously.

He moved off the couch while the man positioned himself on the edge of a green chair and Jack moved his mouth to the man's genitals. He was already quite erect, his glans emerging pink and humid from the tight sheath of his foreskin.

'I don't want to swallow,' he warned. Jack knew he wasn't quite ready for that.

'Sure, mate,' the other said. 'I'll pull out in time, promise.'

He did.

Riding the tube back to his house later, Jack confusedly tried to analyse the recent events. It had not changed his opinion: he knew he still wasn't attracted to men. But he also knew that sucking cock wasn't totally unpleasant.

Which, he supposed, now made him bisexual too.

44

Milduta apologised profusely to Henk for her escapade in Zurich. Blamed it on the way he had made her so unhappy and begged him to be more understanding of her, requesting patience until she could put the pieces of her mind back together. After all, it had been a big shock having the baby and his evident lack of enthusiasm had not helped much, she pointed out to him.

'So, how was it in Switzerland?' Henk finally asked her, after she had put Ivo to sleep and unpacked her clothes. He had watched with puzzlement as she unpacked the numerous new items she had acquired in Zurich, but did not query her further about their origin.

'He was not for me, Henk,' was all she chose to say.

'So we are together again?'

'I not know yet,' she replied.

'Why do you come back here, to Holland, then?' he protested.

'Because Ivo is also yours. You his father and must look after me and little one.'

Henk's eyes clouded over.

'OK,' he agreed.

They had split-pea soup together in the kitchen, a heavy veil of silence hanging between them.

After she had cleaned the bowls in the sink, he went to the closet and brought out a bottle of red wine. In their early days together in the house, it had been a pleasant tradition to share some glasses of wine, following dinner, when they planned to spend the evening in. He visibly wished to make peace with her, she knew.

Before downing the first glass, she felt obligated to tell him the facts of life. Regardless of the mistake she had made by going to live with the other man in Switzerland, she couldn't rekindle her affection for him, not for the time being at least. She stood firm in not wishing to resume their sexual relations.

Milduta established her terms: she would accept the hospitality of his roof only because he was the father of her child, that was all. She would earn her keep, whether she had to return to the biscuit factory or do domestic chores for others; she would cook for the three of them and iron his shirts, but he must look after Ivo for two evenings a week to allow her the opportunity to go out and see friends or whoever she wished. This until the day the local authorities could provide her and the baby with their own accommodation, at which time she would move out. Once away from here, he could visit Ivo whenever he wanted as long as she had sufficient warning. She had no intention of keeping his son from him.

Henk exploded and swept the wine bottle off the table and saw it crashing to the stone floor of the kitchen.

Milduta plain ignored him and walked off to the spare room where she and the baby slept.

As they began to clumsily coexist again, Henk's mood swings became worse. His sister, worried about his sanity and about Milduta and the baby's safety, convinced him to attend a nearby therapist. He only agreed to her suggestion if Milduta accompanied him, as he blamed her for the stress of the situation. For the sake of Ivo, she did. He was officially diagnosed as manic depressive.

Several times, when his frustration would get the better of him, she would have to lock herself in the small room away from his attention, and listen to him ranting on the other side of the door as his drinking got out of control. Some days, it became difficult to avoid his insults and festering resentment and she had to duck on occasions from his feeble attempts to hit her. A few times he succeeded, although he never hurt her badly and would always end up in tears afterwards, apologising wildly between sobs.

'Just once, for old time's sake,' he begged.

'No.'

'Please, Milduta.'

'Never.'

'I haven't changed,' he insisted. 'It's you.'

'It's both of us,' she replied.

Henk insisted.

'Maybe if we have another child together, we could make things work.'

Milduta refused point-blank.

Surely, he couldn't be serious.

45

Milduta remembers the man in London who turned down her offer of cybersex and often made her laugh. He was called Jack, she recalls. Always so polite and thoughtful, unlike most of the other men who had courted her online. The one who called himself 'melancholy'. She has to rummage through a confusion of old papers and out-of-date diaries to find the page where she had noted his e-mail address.

She writes to him, informing him she is now back in the Netherlands, explaining that things hadn't quite worked out as she hoped with the banker from Zurich. She still thinks of Jack warmly, she says. It would be nice if they could chat again.

Jack answers and they resume their conversations, online and over the telephone. He also remembers her fondly and is genuinely surprised she should get in touch again. And delighted.

Gradually, she reveals all the details of her time in Zurich. He sympathises with her, but is amazed by her candour and naivety. How could she have got involved with the weird banker so quickly and trusted him so openly, he asks her?

'I am that sort of girl,' she replied. 'I give people benefit of doubt. Is that wrong?'

'No, it's admirable,' he answered. 'But dangerous. You must be more careful in future, Milduta,' he warned her.

She is now working four mornings a week at the biscuit factory, starting at 6 am with the early shift, bored out of her mind most of the time, increasingly impatient for news from the officials at the town hall about the future availability of a small house in the area. The only fun she has is on the Internet when Henk is away and not using the computer. She makes new friends. One is in Brooklyn, another in New Orleans. They all want her to come to America. There are also lots of other English men. Some wild, some shy, deluging her with sweet obscenities and deliciously improper proposals.

She feels lonely, buried as she is by the grey shield of the flat Dutch countryside and the ever-present morning mist she has to cycle through in all weather to reach the factory.

Jack and she begin tentative conversations about actually meeting in real life. He is aware that her situation in the house she has to share with Henk is becoming increasingly delicate. She has no secrets from him any longer, although she has always kept her sexual activities back in Estonia safely in the dark. It's all now part of another life and she sees no point reviving a past that already feels so distant.

Jack counsels caution. He hasn't informed Milduta of his setback with Rachel the previous year.

'You not want see me, Jack?'

'I do, Milduta. I do. But let's not plan this too much, raise expectations too high.'

'I see.'

'I will come to Holland, it's agreed. I'm just waiting for the right opportunity. Trust me.'

'Is OK.'

'Listen, Milduta, I don't expect sex, you know. I don't want you to think that it's going to be like with Max all over again,' Jack warns her. 'We'll just meet, have a drink, enjoy a nice meal together, see how we feel. No obligations for either of us, OK? Maybe we will only become good friends. Platonic, you see?'

'Is good,' Milduta typed.

And it was true; Jack couldn't help but hope for more when he finally came face to face with this strange Estonian girl and her crazy, upside-down values, but he wasn't counting on it. Too much realism coursing through his veins, along with his innate pessimism.

There was a large international book fair taking place in Warsaw a few weeks later. It was not an event he had to attend, but he felt he needed an alibi of some sort, so that he could justify the trip as more than a pretext to see Milduta. Jack made arrangements with his travel agent to stop over in Amsterdam for one night and day on his way to the Polish capital. Through the web, he found himself a small hotel close to the main railway station, overlooking one of the minor canals that criss-crossed the city. He booked himself a room, insisting on a king-size bed as a contingency.

His plane landed mid afternoon and he took the shuttle into town and walked to the hotel, which he found easily. The room turned out to be surprisingly small and on the ground floor, with passers-by on the pavement outside at eye level with the bed when the curtains were not drawn.

He had a walk down Kalverstraat, checking the shelves of American book imports at the Atheneum, browsing at the pornography on liberal display in the plethora of sex shops crowding the area, and discovered to his surprise that a small indie record store he had visited almost a decade earlier was still in the same location; he treated herself to a boxed set of Philip Glass opera music and unhurriedly made his way back to the hotel room.

They had agreed to meet for dinner. Milduta couldn't make it any earlier, as she had to wait for Henk to get home from work to look after Ivo for the evening.

She had lied to Henk that she was visiting the ballet in Amsterdam with some of the girls from the factory and would be having a drink with them afterwards. She would be staying with one of them to avoid waking Ivo and him up on her return.

He had just nodded indifferently. Not that Milduta even cared whether he believed her or not. This was one of her free evenings, anyway.

46

She is so much taller than he expected. Somehow, he'd forgotten one of their first chats in which she might have mentioned the fact.

Conversely, she finds him shorter than she had mentally imagined. Odd how height is seldom conveyed by photographs with any degree of accuracy. He excuses himself by pointing out that past the age of 40 men begin to shrink ever so slightly. Too many years of wasted sperm and all that. Which makes her laugh.

Actually, they are more or less the same height.

She is also prettier than her photographs.

There is a delicacy about her, a gravity and gentle sadness which, allied to the charm of her accent and that ever-present smile so full of gentleness, makes Jack feel shy like a reborn schoolboy. They greet each other in the lobby of his hotel with a chaste kiss.

'So, here we are!'

'Yes.'

'No problem getting away from home?'

'No.'

Milduta's hair is shorter and has ash-blonde streaks. Her eyes are wonderfully pale, swimming between shades of blue and grey. She is wearing an elegant two-piece black suit with discreet embroidery highlighting its sleeves and borders. The skirt reaches her knees. She has nice legs, and a notably high waistline and strong, child-bearing hips. The jacket is buttoned over a black silk shirt, through which the imperceptible trace of her bra draws a thin line. In the harsh light of the lobby, Jack notes that her suit has seen better days; a shiny patch there, a frayed edge there.

It's windy outside, a strong breeze rising from the banks of the canal where bicycles are parked in a tidy row.

'I'm hungry. What about you, Milduta?'

'Yes, would be nice to eat quickly.'

'We could go straight to eat. Have drinks in the restaurant. Save us from walking any longer than we need to in this cold.'

'OK,' she agrees.

'You're my local guide. Where do you wish to go eat?'

Milduta, who seldom visited Amsterdam, had only vague memories of restaurants in the area and they drifted a bit around the town centre until Jack finally spotted a French restaurant with warm lights in a street near the Dam and decisively suggested they alight there.

The meal came and went quickly as the couple plunged into an endless conversation about everything and nothing. There was so much to talk about. Things they couldn't discuss online or over the telephone. Milduta showed him photos of little Ivo and he recognised the sheer pride in her eyes. She also had pictures of herself in Estonia when her hair fell down over her shoulders and had been much darker, no doubt its natural colour. He much preferred her now, he admitted. Thinking that the pain she had recently endured had turned her into a woman, no longer a superficial young girl, although that angelic, if mischievous, smile had always been present, he noticed.

They had been seated at a small corner table upstairs in the restaurant, and their meal together was partly spoiled by the boisterous presence of a party of office workers in a celebratory mood at a large table on the other side of the mezzanine. From time to time, Jack noticed the curious way some of the crowd at the other table looked over at them, maybe guessing the illicit nature of their encounter or disapproving of their obvious age difference, or it could just have been the fact that they spoke softly in English in a bid for privacy.

Following the meal, they roamed the cold streets of the city centre for an hour, the subject of his hotel room deliberately left unsaid. They skirted the red-light district, which visibly fascinated her. She even mentioned the fact that she had sometimes even thought of selling herself to men, if only to know what it might feel like. Jack frowned in evident disapproval. She had a child now, she pointed out, what could she do? Maybe, she reflected, she should take an advertisement and find herself a rich lover who would house her somewhere in exchange for occasional servicing; the rest of her time would be hers, wouldn't it? Jack pointed out that it didn't quite work like that. Milduta grinned. He wasn't sure whether she was having him on or not.

She insisted they find this famous condom shop she knew about, in a street which ran parallel to the main canal. It was closed of course, as the time approached midnight; a brightly lit window, full of almost a thousand varieties of condoms in all shapes, sizes and colours. Jack found it all rather underwhelming but it cheered Milduta up after her morose and dangerous daydreaming of prostitution.

He knew that her last train back to Henk's countryside house had by now long departed. He took her hand in his. She didn't resist. And slowly began walking back in the direction of his hotel.

They walked in silence now.

The lobby was below street level and access to the rooms was by a small lift. He didn't specifically ask her up, but she quietly followed him into the lift.

The door to the room closed and Jack hung up his coat. Milduta just stood there. He slowly moved his lips towards hers and they kissed. She tasted like bliss.

She remained standing on the edge of the narrow bed as he proceeded to undress her with slow deliberation, slipping off her flimsy panties and burying his nose and mouth into the short, matted hair of her cunt. Her heat radiates outwards. She thrilled on the edge of silence to the firm but gentle caress of his tongue, opening her up.

She came.
Jack was still fully dressed.
He tore his own clothes off and they moved onto the bed.

47

Her body is pale and her breasts slight.

'34B', she confesses.

He stretches out above her, extends his arm towards the window and pulls a gap in the curtains together. The cold from outside is seeping into the room and they both have goose bumps, lying there on the bed's roughly patchworked cover. But they feel no need to slip in between the sheets quite yet.

Skin adheres to skin in search of mutual warmth.

Her hips are high and firm, like a Russian peasant's he fleetingly imagines, flesh taut against the bone.

In the shimmering penumbra of room 107 of the Singel Hotel, Jack surveys the pale expanse of her skin as he delicately spreads Milduta out beneath his own weight, and they embrace with languor; limbs interacting with limbs, outstretched, extremities bent, carefully folded, as they instinctively discover the invisible positions by which they fit against each other long before any act of penetration; the contours that respond to others, the hollows that fit in with the angles, the softness that responds to close contact, all the shapes of a mysterious equation that seems to calibrate the rise of their desire. All the while, their mouths devour each other frantically, with a hunger seemingly born of desperation.

'You kiss good,' Milduta says, drawing back for breath as they part for a moment.

'Thank you,' Jack says.

'No, really...'

'You too.'

He moves back, lies sideways, his elbow supporting his chin. His eyes are now fully used to the dark. He notes every mole and blemish scattered across the whiteness of her skin. A brown stain spreads lazily on the left side of her left breast; a birthmark, no doubt. There is hardened mole in the small of her back, a spot of darker pigmentation blending into the darker pink of her right nipple. A similar one peers indiscreetly through the crowded curls of her pubes, almost extending the sharp line of her vaginal gash. He is not being critical. He knows she would find as many, if not more, minor imperfections liberally scattered across his own body. He just notes all these features which are original to her, recording her body in intimate detail, functioning like a camera; memories for the likely times she will not be by his side, for the days when she will have flown into other arms. He realises already she is a free spirit and that she is not the sort of woman he could ever cage forever, however luxurious and affectionate the hypothetical prison he could build and decorate to harbour her.

He moves back towards Milduta.

He licks every exposed inch of her.

She responds unbidden and devours his cock with unfeigned ardour but also a touching delicacy, her active and clever tongue darting across his shaft, pleasing, teasing, tasting, mapping every contour of his hardness. Her hot mouth moves down and cups and then swallows his heavy, dark balls, weighing them with her ever mobile tongue. Her lips impulsively manipulate his cock; she does not use her hands there, grabbing his arse cheeks and holding them gloriously apart with her fingers as she works his penis with artistry.

She is so good, he notes. An early-warning wave sweeps through his body and he shrugs and moves back from her, indicating further servicing of his cock is no longer required, let alone recommended. Jack does not wish to come in her mouth or against her.

Their bodies move close together again and they resume their embrace. Her mouth still tastes of his cock.

As he caresses her idly, he sees her nipples are not overly sensitive. She had warned him of this during the course of their chats. Her Achilles heel, she'd said.

'Now,' Jack proposes.

'OK,' Milduta acquiesces.

'How do you prefer it?'

'Doggie style,' she whispers quietly, a tremulous tone in her voice. He's not sure whether she has blushed slightly or not. The heat from her body reaches him with unseen ripples of lust carried within its silent stream.

He turns her over, holds his cock aloft and directs it to her entrance. Her shady sex lips are already slightly parted, separated by thin slivers of moisture. The view from his vantage point as he settles on his knees to be at her level is breathtaking: the puckered hole of her anus is darker, staring at him; inviting, vulnerable. He wonders if she has ever been taken there. He positions himself at her lower opening, parts her now dripping wet labia with his fingers as Milduta responds with no need of words and raises her rump further upwards, her face buried into the blankct, her small breasts hanging firmly from her supple body.

Jack thrusts himself into her.

Invests her cunt.

Her insides are on fire, warming his cock in a cloak of heat.

Milduta holds her breath as he plunges into her depths and exhales with a deep sigh of pleasure.

It is done. They are now lovers.

48

Jack would later reflect how much Milduta enjoyed taking her pleasure. There was no holding back as her whole body just surrendered to the moment, spasms coursing hedonistically in slow motion through her, reflecting outwards from her cunt to all the distant poles of her flesh; every inner circuit and synapse in overdrive as the wave swept over her soul and took full possession of her, epileptic and staccato movements moving the muscles in her stomach up and down, her fingers gripping the material of the sheets, her pale eyes wide open in wonder and amazement.

He surprised her in the morning by sliding down between the sheets now sheltering their nude bodies and waking her with his tongue and the gentle pressure of his teeth inside her still moist cunt, in which he could still taste himself. She came like a torrent, surprising him with the sheer violence of her orgasm. Maybe it was the element of surprise. Most of the women he had known previously were in the habit of washing themselves after a fuck; Mimi was the first since Edwina not to do so and keep his spent juices inside her.

He savoured the way Milduta's whole being tensed as if shocked by electricity as she came and she greedily savoured every cell of her pleasure with teeth clenched and body relaxed a point of weightlessness. Looking up from her cunt, Jack sought her eyes in the growing light seeping into the room. It was raining outside; he could hear the pitter-patter of the water against the windowpane and the sound of the town's traffic awakening in the distance.

Her pupils were dilated and the pale colours of her soul appeared to be talking to him in some invisible language, begging... for what?

He pulled himself up and smothered her nakedness with the whole of his body, his hard cock digging into her stomach. He adjusted himself, pushed her legs apart and inserted himself between her swollen cunt lips. He slid in effortlessly. She was again ready for him.

While he moved in and out of her, her speechless eyes locked on his, imploring, screaming silently, watching him in rapt attention as he fucked her, occasionally wiping an unruly lock away from his forehead as it regularly dislodged itself from his unmanageable mop, both remained wordless.

This was no time for conversation.

Or endearments.

Or talking dirty.

That would come later.

Something about Milduta, this strange combination of passivity and unmistakable wanton desire to be used over and over again, touched Jack deeply.

His cock deep inside her brushing against her cervix, he came with a roar, calling out her name. Milduta ran her fingers through his distraught hair. Her first gesture of affection which had not been exclusively sexual until now. He could feel himself shrink inside her, still moistly bathing in his own ejaculate as it settled inside her cunt. Jack wearily closed his eyes and they both dozed off, joined together, for another half hour or so.

Before they finally rose for breakfast, he surprised himself by managing another erection as he watched the soft, firm globes of her arse move majestically from bed to toilet and back. And listened to her pee as she left the door wide open.

Noting his arousal on her momentary return, Milduta squatted down next to him and took his still unwashed cock into her mouth and promptly sucked him off to completion, his thin, tired come jetting into the hospitable cavern of her cheeks. She said nothing and afterwards rose quietly to walk again to the bathroom where he overheard her spitting out his come and gargling.

'How do I taste?' he joked when she returned.

'Acceptable,' she said, with the trace of a smile on her dry lips.

He took his turn in the bathroom and washed and shaved. While he was brushing his teeth, Milduta, who had by now dressed, put her face round the door and watched him clean the lather away from his ears and neck. Jack stood naked at the sink.

'I not been with many cut man,' she remarked, looking down at his dangling cock.

'Cut?'

'You know, with skin around penis gone?'

'Oh, circumcised...' he acknowledged, 'glad I was a novelty!'

'Is true it feel less sensitive there when is no skin to protect?' she inquired.

'I don't know, Milduta. I have no way to compare.'

She burst out laughing and he kissed her tenderly.

He just couldn't get over the fact that she kept her eyes open all the way throughout their lovemaking. It affected him deeply. He didn't know why.

A silent stare that spoke of a thousand words.

And how she joked over her cereal and milk later at a nearby cafe that her eyes must now be all shiny and glazed, and that Henk would know without the shadow of a doubt what she had been up to. That she had been fucked. Some things, she insisted, she could not hide from people who knew her well. What they had done last night and still this morning was written all over her face and would remain there for days.

She quickly reassured Jack by stating that it didn't matter in the least. Her body, her life, and it had been good, she added.

'Really.'

'I'm so pleased.'

'I not regret.'

'Neither do I, Milduta. Although I must say I hadn't truly expected we would sleep together on our first meeting. It felt presumptuous to even assume it before I came to Amsterdam.'

'You too complicated, Jack. I know we fuck. I know you be good lover.'

Jack called for the bill.

Milduta remained with him the whole day as they explored Amsterdam together, his guide to the city on this cold and windy December day. They ventured to the new Opera building, the flower market and, ever-hungry after their physical exertions, shared a cheap Chinese noodle-soup meal, where she almost choked on bamboo shoots following an unremarkable joke of his that set her roaring with laughter.

They returned to his hotel, fucked again, slowly, tenderly, before the time came for him to vacate the room and travel to the airport for the flight to Warsaw, while she had a train to catch.

They parted at the railway station where they had trains on different platforms. Both hated emotional partings and their separation was quiet and dignified, lacking in any kind of future promises.

As her carriage pulled away, Jack reflected on his vision of her in the throes of sex, the expression on her face, her deep blue eyes, the sublime and utterly pornographic spectacle of her raised rear as he had plowed in and out of her.

Nervously facing the prospect of confronting Henk and looking forward to holding her child in her arms again, Milduta felt cheerful that her impulsive encounter had been with a man who was capable of making her laugh with his dry, almost absurd, jokes and wit.

She had no regrets. Sex was good and, after all, she wasn't born to be a nun, was she?

49

Milduta had spoken to Jack about many of her dreams and her unformed plans for the future.

She knew she couldn't remain under Henk's roof much longer.

The strain was getting to her and she feared for her safety as his depression worsened with every look of rejection she granted him and the fact that her physical presence so close to him couldn't help but revive the seething embers of his past passion. His patience would inevitably break and she or Ivo would become a hapless victim of his anger.

She had seriously thought of advertising herself in some magazine or other as a potential mistress for a rich man to subsidise and keep in comfort. After all, it was only sex she would have to provide in exchange, and some companionship. And she gave this away for free anyway, if only to keep sane. And the fact that she enjoyed it. So, she estimated, it would merely be a commercial transaction. Nothing as compromising or as morally reprehensible as prostitution. She held to her logic. She wasn't a whore, and never would be, however much the sight of those women in the red-light district, sitting in their windows in revealing attire, fascinated and aroused her in dubious ways.

Seeing how Jack's eyes had clouded over, when she had jokily revealed her thoughts to him over breakfast that morning after, betrayed his helpless disapproval so Milduta had quickly dismissed the whole idea as a joke.

But she did put a discreet advertisement in the newspaper a fortnight later.

And placed a differently worded notice in a contact magazine she had fortuitously come across, catering for lonely men. Company for dinner, she offered. No fees involved, just a substitute for loneliness.

Within a week, her postbox rapidly filled with a couple of handfuls of responses to her advertisements. She had extra prints of her photo in Nijmegen Castle made. She knew she appeared serious as well as attractive in that shot. Not some cheap girl on the make from the old Soviet Republics.

Her Dutch wasn't good enough for a sustained correspondence, nor was her written English, so she would send the photograph to those suitors who appeared safe, together with her cellphone number.

She operated likewise with the men she encountered in the Internet chat rooms who seemed to have more conversation than others and didn't uniquely wish to share hollow cybersex with her, or talk pruriently through their sexual experiences, or question her in much intimate detail about hers – although she had to admit shamefully to herself that she was undeniably attracted to certain guys who provided evidence of a particularly fertile, if not depraved, form of imagination. Fortunately, most seemed to be far away in America and thus unavailable for temptation.

Cautiously at first, she began to meet some of the men she was making contact with.

A drink in a public place, maybe a meal if they seemed decent, at worst a blow job if she deemed them unremarkable or unsuitable, just to make them feel wanted and not gain the impression of an evening totally wasted. What was the harm in that?

It kept her out of the house for a few hours; always looking after the little one in that stifling atmosphere, dodging Henk's clutches.

She knew she was capable of controlling any situation before matters became dicey. She could handle the sheer predictability of men and their repetitive demands.

And in most instances, it would go no further than a pleasant meal. The majority of the men she met seemed too scared to even suggest the possibility of sex or further contact beyond that evening, and remained quite content to recite their life stories, open up their sadness to her, exorcising their emptiness in the presence of a pretty woman.

One factory owner from Delft actually made a business offer to set her up as his mistress, but she detected something askew about him and declined his generous offer. Maybe he reminded her too much of Max, the Zurich bank manager. And that lesson was now well learned.

Throughout these months of casual encounters – and meals, she put on an extra three kilos! – she remained in touch with Jack, whose words were always tender and rhapsodised about their night and day in Amsterdam and promised he would one day return.

She met another Englishman.

An export sales representative who travelled continuously across Northern Europe, dealing in electronic systems. He would fuck her in his car, a blue saloon, not even bothering to dine her after their initial meet or even take her to a hotel room, but somehow she kept on seeing him several times and allowing him use of her body. He was using her, she realised, and in her mind, she accepted this as a form of necessary punishment, penance for the desolate state of her life. She thought of the rep as 'the asshole', but every time he called her on the phone that he would be passing through Holland, she agreed to a meeting. Afterwards, after he'd moved on, she would cry. Not because of any pain, although he was rough and fucked her quite hard, but because she knew that as he treated her like dirt, she also took surprising pleasure from his uneducated thrusts and animal dominance. Why was sex with the asshole a form of penance, she wondered, her mind in a frenzy of contradictory feelings and emotions?

She confessed about this ongoing affair to Jack, in London. Told him all the sordid details of their meetings and the way the man obliged her to surrender her dignity. Milduta knew her revelation would bruise his soul, but he absolved her.

So she consented to see the jerk again.

He drove her to a sparse forest, a half-hour's drive from Utrecht. They parked by the side of the motorway and entered the wood until they reached a clearing. The ground was covered with rotting, wet, autumn leaves.

This time, he didn't even bother to undress her; he ordered her skirt up above her waist, roughly pulled her thong off, snapping the elastic in the process and, looking at Milduta, who had remained silent since she had been picked up by him at the local rail station, pointed at a thin patch of grass below an ancient tree whose branches spiralled out towards the low, grey sky.

She could hear the roar of the cars on the road just a few hundred metres away. If anyone had parked by their car, they would have seen her moving, exposed and bottomless, to the ground in the shadow of the dark Englishman.

Slapping her rump, he positioned Milduta on all fours, loosened his belt, pulled his cock out and savagely entered her with no preliminaries. He grunted as he came, then, pre-texting an important business appointment nearby, excused himself from dropping her back at the station where he met up with her and left her standing there, holding her loose knickers up as best she could, speechless, in the clearing, his come still dripping down her thighs and legs.

Never again, she swore to herself right then. But, deep inside, she was already uncertain how long her resolve not to see the asshole again would last.

She uneasily made her way towards the road, with the dubious prospect of having to hitchhike her way back to Henk's house, mentally speculating that maybe she attracted this awful humiliation at some fundamental level; that it was part and parcel of her psychological make-up. A thought that

burned all the way down to her gut but that also brought
sorrow to her heart.

50

Jack would call her at least once a week, telling her repeatedly how much he missed her and liked her and how it had just felt so natural and comfortable being in her company. And not just in bed, he added.

He rarely noticed her online these days.

Apparently, Henk had guessed she was using the computer for her own purposes and had blocked her free access to the Internet and the various forums she frequented, and she was unable to guess the password he had adopted.

Milduta agreed that they had been real good together, at ease with each other as they walked by the Rijksmuseum, the windy canals, Kalverstraat, where the nice department stores were and where he had bought her the new Metallica live double CD and a selection of opera arias featuring the tune from Delibes' *Lakme* that she had been humming repeatedly from distant memory. They had roamed all across the town's centre as time passed swiftly by and dodged bicycles and pedestrians, hand in hand.

They both recalled with a smile the large bay window of the condom shop and its absurd array of colours, shapes and patterns; laughing at the idea of him, or for that matter any man, having to wear such gaudy, protective skins that could glow in the dark or, as he had joked, even speak several foreign languages without deflating. Even how she had forgotten, when they fucked, to get him to actually wear one. Fortunately, she reminded him, she was on the pill, even though it sometimes affected her complexion.

'But it feels better without a condom, doesn't it?'

'Yes, is make you feel much closer together. More feelings. Is more natural,' she had agreed. 'And I confidence you be clean; no diseases.'

Or, how she had pointed out to him some of the features of the red-light-district, while giggling compulsively to conceal her own nervousness and covert attraction: the heavily made-up women in their elevated windows, the closed curtains behind which couples were mechanically copulating, the sex clubs advertising live sex shows.

'You think you could ever fuck on stage, with all people watching you?'

'I'm not sure, Milduta. I'd certainly feel very self-conscious.'

'I sometimes have fantasy of it,' she revealed. 'Or I dream and I wake up very wet in-between legs.'

'Interesting fantasy.'

'Maybe I'm exhibitionist,' she had said. 'But in my dream, I always hear woman in front row say I have pimple on my ass. Is not good.'

They kept on reliving the memories of their brief time together, until it became clear they needed new ones. But Jack couldn't leave London for a while because of pressing business commitments.

But they must meet again, they concurred. Soon.

She had told him, as they both rested between fucks on the narrow hotel bed and he was gazing dreamily at the curls crowning her cunt, how the man in Zurich had insisted she shave her sex. Her pubic hair had just grown back and was curlier than before, she revealed. He had offered to trim her. She had declined.

Back in London, Jack slept badly. The recurring, insistent thought of Milduta's shaven crotch obsessed him and kept him awake, and hard, at night.

She had a lovely cunt. Her dark curls, shining with the wetness of her perspiration, framing the darker curtain of her thick sex lips, pouting through the growth. When she had placed herself on hands and knees with her rear thrust towards him, the spectacle of her partly gaping cunt was better than any porn movie. Her straight pink gash a window into her scarlet inner walls; her opening punctuated lower down by small hills of darker, protruding, puffy islands of flesh which he liked to play with, chew on, pull and stretch gently, opening her glorious cunt like an envelope or a flower, unveiling the nacreous texture of her humid insides.

Fixing that wonderful image on the screen on his mind, Jack, in his empty bed, would move his hand down to his cock and circle his shaft until all the blood was trapped there and he would jerk off manically until his dry cock began to hurt, ever-delaying the moment of release and imagining himself deep inside Milduta.

Then again, mounting her in the missionary position had been as arousing, if only because of the tragic spectacle of her open eyes, full of supplication and vulnerability.

Damn, the girl shook him to his very foundations.

And he well knew she just shouldn't; she was uneducated, a bit of a tramp with dubious morals and a checkered past, and heavily distorted East European values shaped by poverty and ignorance. Worse, she liked heavy metal-music and was a sucker for new-age theories; theorising just the other day on the phone that she was convinced they must have known each other in a previous life, when she was maybe a whore or a slave of some sorts, hence her appetite for sex and humiliation in matters carnal. She hadn't specified what he might have been in his earlier incarnation: slave master, pimp or possibly even a dog.

Oh, why her? he sighed, feeling all the old wounds surface again inside his heart, emotions he thought he had banished for good, consigned to the graveyards of personal history.

Jack didn't wish to face the hurt again.

51

Through her advertisement, Milduta met a young Dutchman, a junior executive for a large electronics multinational group. One of the rare men she had come across over the last few years who was actually in her age group. He appeared gentle and genuinely still interested in her, once the sex part had come and gone. Not unlike Jack, she realised, but at least he lived in the same country as she did and was more readily available.

She was not particularly interested in how men looked. Good looks and personality seldom went hand in hand, she had come to learn. The more rugged or rough-looking a man was, indicated in her experience that he had more depths to him or basic animal attraction.

Ari was handsome, almost too much so. Close-cropped blond hair and and emerald blue eyes, high cheekbones and dark eyebrows, slim but broad shouldered, he was a picture of health, always snug in designer jackets – Armani or Ralph Lauren, as he annoyingly enjoyed pointing out. The only designer wear Milduta had ever owned was a second-hand pair of CK jeans. But, initially, there appeared to be something more lurking discreetly behind his seductive and cajoling exterior. A form of kindness, a soul not tarred by vulgarity or the need to degrade her.

He also liked Ivo and would sometimes pick them up at weekends and take mother and son on long drives through the countryside, where the little boy would marvel at the sight of trains racing by in parallel to the road. 'Train' and 'choo choo' were in fact amongst his first words.

Ari didn't mind the fact she had a child and she couldn't always leave him behind when they arranged to meet; when Henk let her down by intent or forgetfulness.

Following their drives, they would help Ivo fall asleep, still excited as he was by his eventful ride in the car, the sight of so many trains and the sharp, cool air of the flat Dutch plains. Once he was tucked in on the deep settee in the front room, and furniture arranged by its side to keep him from tumbling off, Milduta and Ari would make their way to the bedroom of his bachelor apartment.

After they had been together a few times, Ari gifted Milduta with an old computer he was no longer using and she was able to connect again to the Internet. She missed her naughty conversations and fun there. She lied to Henk that she had saved enough to acquire it herself.

The first time Ari had undressed in her presence, her jaw had dropped when she had caught sight of his penis and its size. He was already tall and strong, but his member appeared enormous and so out of proportion with the rest of him. He noticed her stare and blushed.

'It frightens you?'

'No,' Milduta replied. 'But is really very big one.'

'I'll be gentle,' he said.

And he was.

She was at first nervous that his cock, both long and thick and so much more real than the monstrous cocks she would sometimes discover when she surfed the net, would stretch her and prove painful, but he surprisingly fitted inside her like a glove, once he had sufficiently lubricated her with vaseline or KY jelly to enable the initial penetration. She felt so full, but the sensation was pleasant.

While he was moving inside her, her mind would sometimes wander filthily and try to imagine what it would feel like if Ari entered her rear, and the cinematic image of his oversize cock digging deep into her anal canal would stimulate her feelings of both pleasure and shame. But he was conservative in his sexual tastes and never tried to take her there. And neither did she suggest it.

Despite, or because of, his remarkable size, he would very often have major difficulties in reaching his orgasm, and would thrust away inside her for what seemed like ages, ever on the brink of coming, until her insides felt stirred and raw and she would lose all sensation in her vagina, let alone the tingling electricity of pleasure. Every time she indicated he should maybe withdraw and give up, Ari would insist on being given some moments more inside her, most times to little avail. The fucking became so monotonous and mechanical that she stopped looking forward to it.

On occasions, overcome with mild pity for his dilemma, she would consent to take him inside her mouth after he had pulled out of her, still unspent. It made little difference and she would end up tiring herself out, her head bobbing up and down over his jutting cock until her jaw literally ached from accommodating his unusual bulk in its vain search for climax.

Not only was fucking him becoming a painful chore, but Milduta soon tired of Ari's personality and manners. It wasn't as if he was ashamed of her and hid her away; far from it. He openly considered her to be his girlfriend and enjoyed when she was able to join him and his friends in bars and restaurants. But the novelty and the sense of belonging in a relationship were quickly overshadowed by the fact that, when others were present, he painfully ignored her and his conversations were all tedious monologues about his brilliant career and the constant idolatry of money. For Milduta and her Baltic background, money was merely a means to an end. If she had it, she spent it; she would worry tomorrow if she hadn't any. But Ari and his friends were obsessed by a never-ending desire for more money and hypothetical fortunes. Milduta felt ill at ease in their company.

The next time he called suggesting they get together, Milduta pretexted an excuse and promised to call him back the following week.

She never did. Maybe scarred by his obvious physical inability to achieve orgasm when with her, Ari never manifested himself again

She would often regret their parting over months to come, as he had been the only man she had gone with who had also enjoyed the company of Ivo.

52

Still, like a curse infecting his illogical and captive mind, Jack remembers Milduta.

Her eyes, inches away from his, observing his own features with deft attention as he moves inside her, alternately slow and tender and then hard, rough and lustful. Calibrating his assault according to every minute vibration and variation in her responses; a hiccup, a sigh, a trembling, a sheen of sweat spreading across her forehead and flat stomach.

She watches him, his features contorted by the rising assault of his desire.

She judges him.

She silently asks too many questions he has no answer to.

She listens to the shortness in his breath as his climax approaches, wave after wave of welcome and uncontrollable sensations racing through his straining body.

Her inner lust, her satisfaction, are unmistakable as her eyes mist up with joy, grow weirdly shiny and luminous as she surrenders wholesale to the peculiar strength of her orgasm.

Those eyes, still the colour of a faraway sea lost over the horizon. Moving between the one hundred possible shades of grey and blue with every additional movement of his cock inside the boiling cauldron of her intimacy.

Milduta's eyes.

She has him under her thumb.

53

Jack and Milduta agreed to meet again.

He sent her the necessary money for the train journey to Paris' Gare du Nord by Western Union. They arrived on separate trains from, respectively, London Waterloo and Amsterdam, just a half-hour apart. After disembarking from the Eurostar, he had enough time to get himself an espresso and visit the newsagents on the main concourse and pick up a few recent French literary magazines.

He had booked them into a small, picturesque hotel on the Left Bank, just a stone's throw from the Place de L'Odeon. The room had an unrestricted view of Paris roofs straight from an old movie, and migrating pigeons buzzing and purring outside.

In the taxi from the railway station, she said little and Jack felt shy all over again as if this were the first time. They were evidently both nervous. He suggested she just stand by the side of the bed while he slowly undressed her, garment by garment, a scene he had long rehearsed in his mind. They hadn't even yet unpacked their cases. She wore matching blue cotton underwear, modest, almost schoolgirl-like. He made delightful reacquaintance with her mouth, cradled her small breasts, and lowered her glorious nudity on to the bed and swiftly shed his own clothing in readiness to fuck her.

'Not like this,' Milduta said, as he placed her down on her back and slipped out of his pants.

'How?'

'Doggie style. I feel like. I like more.'

He knew he would miss her the heartbreaking spectacle of

her eyes peering at him throughout the act, but also knew there would be further opportunities during the course of the three days they had planned to be together.

She turned onto her knees and offered him her rear.

Their time together flew quickly past.

They walked a lot, shopped – he bought her a pair of jeans and a short skirt she coveted in a window front – ate too much, caught art films, explored Paris and its obligatory attractions: the Champs Elysées, where all she could somehow hear were the voices of other Russian tourist; the rising steps of the Sacré Coeur in Montmartre; the Eiffel Tower, which she declined to climb, confessing to a fear of heights; the cafes of Montparnasse; the Beaubourg Centre.

They even managed to make love three of four times a day, between walks and visits, finding refuge and warmth at regular intervals in their small room that by now smelled of unbridled lust. Oh, how they fucked with loose abandon, when their stomachs weren't too bloated with all the delicate food they had been eating.

After they'd enjoyed ice-cream and tea at the Häagen-Dazs terrace on the Boulevard Saint Germain and were aimlessly orbiting back towards their hotel, Jack cracked a harmless joke occasioned by the moment and something she had said, and Milduta burst out laughing so hard she couldn't help peeing slightly in her knickers. Back in the room, he religiously licked her cunt lips clean with his tongue. She was still laughing. Jack could feel the onset of joy deep within as the unrestrained sound of her happiness alleviated his own ingrained sense of darkness.

But the long weekend soon came to an end. Milduta had left Ivo with a friendly neighbour and had to be back in Holland that evening.

They returned to the Gare du Nord in embarrassed silence and their second encounter ended there and then, with smiles and too many words left unsaid.

They took their different trains back to their own countries; separate trains and separate lives.

His allocated seat on the late afternoon, Sunday Eurostar placed him next to a young blonde woman. She worked for BBC radio and the conversation flowed easily between Jack and her. He lied, naturally, about the reasons for his Paris trip, although he guessed that the raw smell of sex probably still permeated his breath, clothes and body. The blonde, Jocasta, had been with friends and shopped to exaggeration, as the Galeries Lafayette and Printemps holders stuffed above the seat betrayed. They had pleasantly exchanged cards and promised to make contact again. There was no doubt, Jack could perceive from Jocasta's smile and words, she was willing to date him. The signs were obvious. They shared similar intellectual tastes and media background. But Jocasta held no interest for him. Before Milduta he would have readily agreed to dinner that same evening and probably bedded her.

As he alighted at Waterloo and queued for a taxi, Jack imagined what Milduta was up to right now. Probably biking home from her own local station, her small suitcase strapped in precarious equilibrium to her wheel guard. About to see her son again and confront Henk.

In his own bed that night, he recalled their moments together under his mental microscope, or was it a film projector?

He knew from their brief time in Amsterdam how much she was partial to words and whispers, indecent suggestions and dirty deeds murmured in her ear as they fucked. The way her whole body strained under the impact of his rampant cock as strongly as she reacted to his suggestive words, and her cheeks would colour even deeper at the thought of the stories or scabrous situations he was deliberately outlining. He intimated at another man possibly coming to join them in their carnal activities, and how Jack would vicariously watch the stranger mount her while Milduta was busy sucking him off and every thrust of the other man inside her would push her forward, impaling her mouth deeper onto Jack's cock. How later, both males would simultaneously invest her closely dilated holes. On another night he had improvised a wild story of excess galore in which they were staying by the sea, in the Mediterranean, and under cover of darkness were both kidnapped by pirates or gangsters and turned into sexual slaves for the privilege and enjoyment of their captors. First they had to perform sexually with each other on a raised table whilst being watched and menaced by punishment of a terrible nature should their ardour weaken. Which inevitably happened. At which time, leashes were tightened around their necks and Jack was forced to suck to hardness the oversized cocks of his masters and then have to manually guide the straining, erect penises into Milduta and, bound, be obliged to spectate helplessly as their cruel, male captors despoiled her repeatedly; to cap it all, once they have tired of her and she lays there in a pool of sweat and come and tears, he is then himself sodomised in her presence and had to gladly sacrifice his anal preserve out of pure love and affection for her, to purchase her proffered freedom. She liked that crazy, improvised story, he knew, slipping a sharp-nailed finger into his arsehole as she acknowledged her excitement. She kept on listening in rapt silence as the tale unfolded, but the intense heat generating from her body, her cunt, her skin, betrayed the force of her lust and her eyes acknowledged the charge of her increased excitement.

The words spoke to the slut in her.

And the one lurking in Jack's heart.

54

Jack wants her again.

Badly.

By now, she has finally left Henk's house and lives alone with her growing child in a small cottage owned by the local authorities, just three miles away from Henk's, in a neighbouring village. She is elated by her new-found freedom, and spends hours decorating and repainting the house in pastel colours and bringing the garden back to life.

Henk visits most days to see Ivo. Their conversations are painful and strained. His eyes brood with anger and resentment. After a further outburst full of bile, Milduta refuses him further access to her cottage after dark, fearing another attack or worse. She find a local lawyer who sends her ex a letter of warning to that effect. Two nights later, Henk is standing outside her windows, blind drunk, alternately vehemently shouting at her and pleading his case with genuine tears in his eyes. She turns a blind eye.

A distant family friend arrives from Estonia to spend several weeks in the West and Milduta agrees to accommodate her in exchange for the older woman looking after little Ivo for four or five days, which gives her the opportunity to get a break. She phones Jack in London and announces her availability. He is delighted and makes arrangements.

They meet up in the bright arrivals hall of a small, local airport by the Mediterranean.

She has cut her hair shorter and coloured it a pale shade of auburn. She wears a faded pair of jeans and a burgundy, chenille sweater.

He hires a small car at the Avis counter and they drive an hour to a nearby port town where he has been recommended a pleasant hotel. Their room, all in marine colours and motifs, has a balcony overlooking the sea and as they explore their new surroundings and the incomparable view from the window, Jack can't stop himself from fondling her taut arse restrained by the tight stretch-material of her jeans.

Milduta giggles.

'Oh, sex maniac!'

Jack smiles.

'Of course. How could I not with such a sweet bum at my disposal.'

'You use too many new words for me, Jack,' she says.

'So, let's not talk,' he jokingly suggests. 'We have other things to occupy our time, haven't we?' and kisses her. She melts in his arms.

'Oh, Jack, I not know if ever tell you already, but you are such good kisser...'

'I accept the compliment gracefully, my dear.'

He undresses her with all the slow, lingering ritual of a religious ceremony, renewing his memories of her glorious nudity. He notices how unrestrained her pubic hair has become. Suggests she maybe shaves it, or he do so. She laughs but turns his request down, arguing that she would just sprout awkward pimples there later. But allows him to trim her pubes at least. He breathes in the wonderfully obscene vision of her spread thighs as he works away with his nail scissors.

After their first fuck, they prepare to dress, both by now famished and night falling outside by the nearby shore, with the smell of fish and seafood rising from the parade of restaurants below.

During the course of their frantic lovemaking, he had whispered further tentative improvisations about slavehood and domination and now, mischievously, assumes the role of

Master and, tongue in cheek, forbids her to wear any under-wear for the duration of their stay here. She smiles and gleefully agrees to his whim.

The sheer knowledge of her beckoning nudity and available openings, so close and unprotected beneath the thin fabric of her short dresses, is a major turn-on for the two of them and the short vacation is punctuated by sexual folly as desire over-whelms them both in turn. They eat, they fuck, they talk a lot and neither of them wishes the week to ever end.

One afternoon, quite exhausted from their activities in bed, Jack declares that he needs a short nap and Milduta decides to go for a walk in the town while he rests. Once she is gone, he is unable to sleep and, in her absence, can't help himself from delving into the handbag she left behind. He discovers a photo-graph of her and another man, a good-looking young man by whose side she is blissfully smiling into the lens of the camera. There is no clue to where they are, as their beaming faces occupy the whole frame of the photograph. Jack knows it is not Henk. Or the English asshole or the Dutch computer guy she has told him about. He guesses she is still seeing other men in the intervals between their encounters. He is not surprised but still pained.

He says nothing to her when she returns later to the hotel room they are sharing.

Jack thinks too much.

He knows it. Wasn't it what Edwina had said about the two of them, lamenting the crippling state of their damaged selves?

He is aware this relationship with Milduta doesn't make sense outside of bed, that it has no future.

She is twenty years younger than him and there is no way he can summon up the mental fortitude to even try and believe he is capable of bringing up another child, even more so that of another man. He knows Milduta likes sex too much and will eventually tire of him.

He also realises she is using him and the sex she grants him is her unethical, if Eastern European, way of paying him back for the gifts, the money, the travel. She takes it all for granted as a normal form of exchange between them.

There is nothing malicious or calculating about it. It just comes naturally to her.

He often awakens at three in the morning – that fatal hour of deep vulnerability – in his bed at home, dreaming of her, fantasising about the warmth and mellow softness of Milduta's body, of time and time again witnessing her being fucked by total strangers in most savage and relentless fashion while he tenderly holds her head in his lap and wipes her feverish brow. He imagines taking her to a nude beach and exhibiting her, displaying her to the unflinching gaze of others, her nipples and sex gash immodestly highlighted by scarlet lipstick, showing off her assets, maybe even piercing her parts in a ceremony of dark initiation, and orchestrating her group ravishing in a pagan ceremony by a night fire, under the benevolent sign of a full moon. Jack plays with himself as he imagines, in uttermost detail, the way Milduta's eyes can't help but betray the sexual pleasure she is experiencing. He pictures her with her erstwhile Dutch lover, he of the uncommonly large penis, and, in intolerable close-up, watches as the monstrous cock buries itself in her raw depths to the hilt, stretching her apart like a piece of uncooked meat.

In dreams, Jack has no shame.

55

A month after their visit to the south of France, Milduta sends Jack a birthday card in which she assures him he is special.

Other men might have her body, she awkwardly writes, setting his mind ablaze, but he is the only one to have her soul. Not a consolation he greets with much enthusiasm.

Jack seeks clarification, hoping her words are merely occasioned by her uncertain grasp of English. He hopes against hope.

He asks frantic questions in his e-mails or over the phone but Milduta is supremely talented in avoiding direct answers, and easily manoeuvres the subject aside.

'You are my treasure,' she says.

A week later, she calls him, obviously disturbed, and asks for a small amount of money.

His initial thought is that she has discovered she is pregnant.

Since Amsterdam they had not been taking any precautions.

No, she had badly budgeted her outgoings and a heavy telephone and Internet-provider bill have left her with insufficient money until her benefits arrive at the end of the month. Never again, she promises.

Relieved by the news, Jack obliges and mails her a few hundred pounds in a registered envelope.

Milduta thanks him warmly.

Christmas comes and Milduta has made arrangements to return to Estonia for the festivities, to see friends and her brother, who now has two children. She cannot afford to fly there so she is getting a lift to the German coast at Kiel to catch a ferry to the Baltic States with a girlfriend who has married a Dutchman and is also returning home. It's a whole day's drive. She hopes Ivo will not be sick on the way. Or on the boat later, where they don't have a cabin reservation.

Even though she hasn't asked him, Jack sends her some more money as an early Christmas gift. He also sends a few toys, models of trains, for her little boy, whom he has never seen outside of the photographs she carries with her.

The two-year-old is gloriously blond and looks more like his errant father than Milduta.

Jack is stuck in London for the year end because of business commitments he cannot escape.

56

Jack misses Milduta like hell.

He wants her with a rage. Even deludes himself that it's not just for the sex but also for the quiet post-coital moments of intimacy and companionship, the ports of silence and contentment that form the cement of any successful pairing. He blindly refuses to accept the reality: the evidence of his illogical infatuation for a girl who just knows how to enjoy life so much better than he does and asks herself few questions, or retreats into new-age claptrap when she has cod philosophical moods.

Since she had left Henk's house to go live on her own, they have fewer contacts. She works days and apparently only ventures online in the evenings when he has other engagements. She can only be reached on her cellphone and, most times he tries, it doesn't appear to be switched on or she doesn't answer.

Milduta is often strangely elusive.

And now that she is back in Estonia on her Christmas break, her mobile appears to be out of reach to his network.

Jack seethes with frustration and longing. Wakes in the morning following almost sleepless nights with aches running through his whole body.

Out of sheer stupidity, he logs on to their familiar Internet forum's chat room and changes his handle from 'melancholy' to 'mimi,f29,holland', which is how she had recently been identifying herself. Within minutes he is being paged from all over. The majority of the men calling (and a scattering of bi females) are clearly just attracted by her reasonably exotic, operatic handle, particularly the American-based callers for whom a European provenance is the occasion of countless 'cool' and 'wow' expressions of delight. As if the Internet had ever been a strictly American preserve! But few of them had visibly conversed with Milduta before. It was easy to establish from the initial (and predictable) questions and lack of familiarity.

It's been months, if Jack believed her, since she had last been online for any length of time anyway; too busy with the decoration of her little cottage and the affair with him.

But some interlocutors clearly know her.

Jack improvises his way through a half-hour on-screen conversation with a loft architect in Brooklyn, who has seemingly extended Milduta an open invitation to come see him in America. Which she visibly hasn't yet turned down. It's quite clear they have also spoken several times over the telephone. He seems quite up to date with much of her intimate life although, to Jack's relief, he doesn't appear to know of his own presence in Milduta's life.

As Jack cautiously probes to unveil any further secrets of what might have occurred between Milduta and the architect, even adopting her broken English and ungrammatical expressions to further the illusion she is actually at this end of the conversation, he is finally rumbled and the other man disconnects.

He compounds his mistake the following day and assumes her Internet identity again. He gets paged by 'from infinity and beyond'. Another man, evidently a closet *Star Trek* fan, who also knows Milduta. Through a slow process of deduction and coy answers and questions, Jack uncovers the fact that she and the man are still in regular contact and even exchanged pre-Christmas text messages of an intimate nature. The guy has just returned from a business trip to Japan and the Far East and wishes to meet her again. Wants to call rather than continue the halting online chat. Jack keeps the conversation going by blundering his way through and pretending, as Milduta, that her mobile phone's battery is running low and that, right now, she can't seem to get calls. Which in Estonia she genuinely can't, should the guy actually try.

Inch by inch, Jack elicits further information from the man.

It quickly becomes apparent Milduta is fucking this guy on a regular basis. In a hotel in a place called Aalmark.

The man evokes, with a distinct lack of elegance, how much he loves the sight of her open arse and the breathlessness of her sexual prowess and reminds her of her agreement to a future threesome, as he wishes (has she agreed to this?) to see her with another woman. He thinks he has found the right girl to join them. Early January, same place as usual, he suggests. He could stop off in Amsterdam on his way to a skiing trip in Switzerland and they could have good fun again.

Jack is lost for words.

He logs off angrily as his interlocutor is still in mid sentence, rhapsodising about what he wishes to do with Milduta next time he has her under him on that bathroom floor. To Jack's shame, he recognises some twisted fantasies he has also wished to explore with Milduta himself.

Is she the one who whispered about these proposed sweet excesses in the other man's ear, preferring to submit to them from him rather than Jack?

The recognition that his own sexual obsessions are far from unique vexes him deeply.

As much as the arrows of jealousy.

57

He knew he couldn't have been the only man in her life.

She was young, she had normal appetites, was no doubt lonely, stuck as she was in her Dutch countryside with a small child in tow and almost penniless, while still in the prime of her sexual life and, then, he was not always available.

It was to be expected, after all.

It was Jack being unreasonable, he knew.

But the smug, superior assurance by 'from infinity and beyond', or whatever his damn name was in real life, that she was a hell of a fuck (in response to Jack's probing question 'are you sure you really like me?') and promising her even further fireworks when they could arrange a meet after Christmas, in the obvious expectation of an enthusiastic response, challenged to the core all Jack's assumptions of what he had been sharing with Milduta. It hurt: his heart, his pride.

It wasn't just that he was no longer the only man bedding her right now; it was also the fact that it now even cast doubt as to whether he had satisfied her sexually all along if a yob like this other guy had also succeeded in raising her lust to such levels. Jesus, it even sounded as if she had allowed him to fist her on one occasion, if Jack had correctly interpreted all the unsubtle allusions of minor perversities between the lines of their illicit and accidental online chat as, adopting the persona of Milduta, he had casually fished for compromising information.

It hurt a lot.

And made him so fucking angry at Milduta.

Between the rage, he mercilessly evoked all the haunting

images of her with others (now he also remembered how she had mentioned in an inconsequential way two others she had met the previous year: a Korean-born local guy she had given some private Russian lessons to and a Dutch garage owner, also called Jack, who was in the throes of a divorce and confessed to love her – maybe she was still seeing them, balancing an active sex life with all of them as opposed to Rachel's virtual game of lies and pretence).

He affectionately recalled how, during the courses of their regular, lazy evening meals on the port by the Mediterranean earlier that same year, she had often remarked on the sexual attractiveness of, one day, a waiter who noticeably limped and, the next day, a waitress who had enjoyed using her poor English while serving them, but otherwise happened to be dreadfully plain in looks. Milduta had said she somehow took pity on them, felt a strong urge to reward them, maybe sexually. Was it a sign of her wanton nature he had somehow ignored in his blindness to the facts of their shaky, one-way relationship? Or maybe she just happened to be unnaturally aroused by having to sit at the restaurant table in that short, flimsy skirt, pulled up to mid-thigh level, her smooth cunt below experiencing the quiet but seductive assault of the sea breeze along its exposed, darker gash.

No, she had definitely considered the idea, he realised; no doubt her mind was still unduly excited by their insistent bedside patter, speculating wildly about a third person joining them for fun and games between the welcoming, if crumpled ,white sheets of the cosy hotel room. Had she not realised he only said those mad things to excite her? Was he himself not aware of the power of words? Of all people, he should certainly not have played with fire in such a manner.

So who was to blame?

Had Jack mistakenly opened her secret doors and tempted her to find her pleasure with others?

Or was she just a slut by nature, or merely a cold-hearted

young woman of dubious morality who did not realise how much she was capable of hurting others?

Maybe, after all consideration, Henk hadn't been such a fool. Come to think of it, Jack had only heard her version of their story. Maybe there was another side.

And what about the Belgian boy who had blithely taken her virginity in Bloomsbury and later lost her? Another fool, or another victim along the path of Milduta's sexual odyssey?

58

Still nursing a peculiar sentiment blending both bewilderment and anger in equal measure, Jack felt the need to confront Milduta. Normally, he would have unleashed a barrage of vengeful e-mails or letters – words came easier to him in print than over the telephone – but he knew he would not receive any specific answer to his meandering questions. Just her usual assurances of his always being her soul mate and that what she did with her body was unimportant as he was the one she kept in her heart, and memories of their past together would never be forgotten. He could almost predict her reaction.

Right now, it wasn't enough.

He turned himself into an investigator and roamed the web for hours. Piecing together her story, he located her now-dead grandparent's address back in Tallinn as he knew she was staying there, since her brother had taken over the lease on the apartment when he had returned to town from his provincial exile. So he now knew where to find her.

He booked himself on the first flight to Estonia. It was a quiet period between Christmas and the New Year and seats were readily available. He packed enough warm clothes for a few days and called a minicab to take him to Heathrow.

Tallinn proved unexpectedly pretty, or at any rate the area in the immediate surround of the hotel he had found at the airport's tourist information desk. The cobbled streets shone with a shimmering beauty and reflected the light of the low-flung moon over the old buildings.

There wasn't even any snow on the ground. Somehow, he had been convinced he would be clumsily wading through sheer mountain banks of snow in the Estonian capital, attracting attention by the uneasiness of his progress. The ambient temperature was cold but invigorating, the air cleaner than back in the West, still uncontaminated by urban exhausts and invisible fumes.

The porter doorman of his hotel found him a map of the city and Jack went off exploring.

Walking tentatively in the direction of the area of town where Milduta had been brought up and where she was now, his mind was fiercely attacked by a welter of conflicting feelings.

He still had the need to angrily confront her with his discoveries.

But then he also was aware of the fact that he had specifically logged on to the chat forum under her name to unveil proof of her betrayal, as if his heart had already known about it and just sought confirmation, the ugly details of flesh and fluids, in order to torture himself further. It was just a sickness he couldn't avoid.

Therefore, he was just as guilty as she was.

But he also felt compelled to hold her tenderly in the cradle of his arms and protect her from the harsh realities of the world and other men. So, she had been unfaithful to him. So what? She had never promised him a vow of chastity. He had never even thought of asking her.

Somehow, something madly unhealthy, buried deep inside his heart or loins, hankered still to share her touching beauty with others, but not this way. If it had to happen, it had to be on his terms. With him approving, orchestrating, organising, present.

Otherwise, the acid flow of jealousy just burnt a deep hole at the core of his being.

He located her building with ease, but it was already dark and he was tired from the flight. He would return early the next day, he decided. Although he had no precise plans as to what he should do or say when he finally came across Milduta again. Especially here in Tallinn, where she no doubt least expected him. She would probably accuse him of spying on her.

Which, of course, was precisely what he was doing, wasn't it?

Whether on the Internet or in Tallinn.

The following morning, Jack kept watch on the grey apartment block's recessed front door and porch for almost half a day, standing patiently on the nearby street corner, his gloved hands digging deep into his coat pockets and a woollen scar draped inelegantly around his neck and chin. His nose and ears were no doubt some strange shade of scarlet, exposed as they were to the bitter cold.

Milduta emerged just after midday.

She held a small boy's hand and haltingly made her way, holding a visibly heavy suitcase in her other hand, towards the nearest bus stop, around the corner of her street. Jack waited until the tramway came, its brakes screeching sharply, and she departed on it, and he then quickly hailed a cab. Asked the driver in sign language to follow her. Where the hell was she going now? He also realised this was the very first time he had seen little Ivo in the flesh. The kid, bundled up in several layers of warm clothing, seemed so tiny and fragile it tugged a heartstring inside Jack. Until now, he had only ever thought of the boy as a potential problem, standing between the two of them and a possible future together. His shuffling gait as he followed his mother onto the tram reminded him of one of the dwarves in the Walt Disney version of Snow White that he had probably seen when he was the same age as Ivo.

59

The tramway pulled up with another protest from its over-worked brakes at a way station close to the port. Jack requested the taxi to stop. Of course, it now dawned upon him, this was the day she was due to return back to the Netherlands. How could he have forgotten? The empire of jealousy had frailed his heart apart and scrambled his damn mind.

He briefly watched Milduta and the small, trailing boy as they first greeted another young woman in thick winter attire who had been waiting for them and, all together, made their way towards the port gates and quickly went through passport control.

He moved closer to the barbed-wire fence and watched them move along to the gangway of a boat moored along the quay and embark, manoeuvring the incline with their heavy cases. He noted the ship's name and rushed to the booking office to check its destination: Kiel.

The clerk automatically asked Jack in English if he wished to purchase a ticket. The boat wasn't sailing for another ninety minutes. Yes, the company certainly took credit cards. Impulsively, having checked his watch, Jack bought a passage to Kiel.

The taxi he had used to follow Milduta and Ivo to the port was still waiting at the rank, close to where he had been dropped off. Jack ordered him back to the hotel where he quickly repacked and settled his bill before making his way back to the port.

By the time he boarded the boat and began seeking his cabin amongst the now thickening throng of returning holiday-makers, he still had over half an hour to spare.

He still had little idea what he would say or do when he for-tuitously bumped into Milduta and the child, once they had sailed. Mentally drained, he fell asleep fully dressed on his bunk within minutes of the departure from the port.

It was dark by the time he awoke. They were at sea, the Baltic coast now quite out of sight. His first thought was to remember he suffered from seasickness. Fortunately, the boat's store was still open and he was able to buy a complement of pills.

He caught a glimpse of Milduta, her girlfriend and the boy at the ship's busy snack bar that evening but decided not to make contact quite yet. Neither did he follow them to find out which cabin they were staying in. Come to think of it, she might not even be staying in a cabin for the crossing, travelling as she was on a limited budget. He noticed the little one holding on to a book about trains as if his life depended on it; it had been a present Jack had sent him.

The man who sent her child books full of pictures of trains. Was that how Milduta thought of him, might remember Jack in times to come?

The following day, for the second and final night of the crossing, the ship held a large dance after dinner and, sitting in a remote corner of the cavernous and shabbily decorated hall, Jack observed Milduta from afar as she warmly kissed little Ivo goodbye, and her friend took the boy's hand and they returned together to the cabin or wherever they were sleeping.

Now alone, Milduta walked over to the bar and ordered a glass of red wine, and she began sipping slowly from her glass as the disco music roared out from the loudspeakers standing at the other end of the big room on the unoccupied stage on which bands of real musicians must have played in better days, but was now just harbouring a disc-jockey booth with a couple of turntables.

The sounds of the music and its insistent beats enveloped the room, prompting older passengers to retreat and younger ones to raise the shrill level of their conversations.

The melodies were formless and loud, an aggregate of frantic rhythms and naked cacophony.

Jack watched as a man detached himself from the milling crowd on the perimeter of the room and walked over to Milduta at the bar and invited her to dance with him. She smiled back radiantly. Damn, why did she always smile so invitingly? Jack retreated into his corner of darkness and watched, with rapt attention, how she swayed so effortlessly on the dance floor, almost oblivious to her partner, dancing as if isolated in her own cocoon of song, her hips swinging softly to the caress of the music. She was a good dancer.

Another drink, then another anonymous dance partner and a turn on the floor.

Midnight came and he could see Milduta was beginning to be affected by the alcohol she had liberally been downing, with every new dance partner eager to gift her with a further round. She had been on vodka for some time now. Her dance steps were now lazy and proved unsteady and visibly less sensual.

But she seemed content, that permafrost smile still revealing the uneven landscape of her teeth, never engaging in any real conversation with any of her brief dance partners, lost in her private thoughts, surrendering to the warmth of the drinks soaking her body and the pleasing feel of music and male attention.

Jack downed his Coca-Cola. It had gone quite flat and tasted awful, its sweetness diluted down by the overload of ice that had come with it. Just like in America or at McDonald's, he reckoned. He watched as Milduta's last dance partner whispered something in her ear and took her by the hand. She didn't resist. The couple moved across the dance floor towards one of the doors that led to the lower deck.

Jack followed, losing time as he had to struggle through the mass of epileptic dancers now shaking up and down to the sounds of a Chemical Bros rave hymn. It had been hours since he had last taken a travel pill and he was feeling distinctly queasy already.

What he saw when he finally emerged into the night, and his eyes grew accustomed to the starlit darkness, didn't help.

There was Milduta, in a far corner of the deck, on her knees, sucking the man's cock with an appetite that appeared mighty indecent. The man gripped her hair between his hands, forcing her to take him even deeper. She showed no sign of resistance.

From his hiding place in the shadows, Jack couldn't make out whether Milduta's eyes were open or not.

In shock, he turned and vomited over the wooden deck.

60

His mouth still full of bile, Jack couldn't tear himself away from the dreadful spectacle of Milduta orally servicing her last dance partner of the evening.

Had he suggested the tryst, or had it been her initiative?

His whole body now shuddered from the cold and the sad inevitability of the sordid porno sequence he was now witnessing. Just a bad movie, with low production values: the sparse deck of a ship, the pale and pasty cheeks of the stranger, a thin sliver of moonlight insufficient for clarity of vision, obscuring the minute details of the sequence unrolling in front of Jack. The man's face harboured a contented smile. Milduta's actions were shadowed, although there was little doubt as to her actions.

There was a moment when, in the advancing penumbra of midnight, Jack noticed the standing man sketching an imperceptible retreat – was he about to come? – but Milduta just impaled herself deeper on his shaft and kept him in her grasp. The man's body visibly shook, with Milduta still intimately joined to him.

Jack, conquering his distaste, guessed he was now filling her throat with his come.

Finally, the man withdrew from her mouth, tucked himself away, mumbled something Jack was unable to hear from his vantage point and moved away slowly from the woman still kneeling at his feet, soon disappearing through a door into the warmth of the boat.

Milduta finally rose.

The silence of the sea was deafening.

Jack held his breath.

His thoughts tumbling inside his brain with all the clamour of despair and helplessness.

Milduta stood for a while, watching the sea unfurl all the way to the dark horizon, lost in her own unknowable thoughts.

What, Jack wondered, could be on her mind now?

Did she feel there was poetry in the landscape of the night? Sadness in the oppressive silence that now surrounded them, broken only by the clapping sound of the nearby waves beating against the ship's metallic hull?

Jack moved towards Milduta.

Her silhouette was highlighted against the brightness of the pockmarked moon.

As gently as he could – he didn't wish to scare her – he lowered a hand onto her left shoulder.

She jumped.

Maybe the other man now wanted more of her?

She turned round to face him.

He realised she was crying.

'You?' she gasped.

'Yes,' he answered, a hard knot gripping his stomach. 'Why the tears? Ashamed of what you have done? Of what you are, deep down inside, Milduta?'

'What are you doing here?'

The faint trace of a dismissive smile spread across her dry, cold lips.

'I'm here. That's all. I came to see you. And then I saw. What else must I say now?'

'You should not have come.'

'I know that now.'

He sighed. A faint breeze was wafting in from the sea. Neither of them wore a coat against the winter night.

'I loved you,' Jack said quietly.

'You never said so before,' Milduta replied. 'Maybe you should have had the courage to.'

'Oh, Milduta, why do you do these things?'

'It's just way I am, Jack. I am not perfect. Is so easy succumb to needs, to cravings. I not always proud, you know.'

'Really?' He couldn't find it in himself to be ironic.

'I'm lost, Jack. I'm lonely. So I do things I regret later. I just lost Estonian girl...'

'I loved you,' Jack senselessly repeated. 'Didn't you ever guess, didn't you even realise it by now, Milduta?'

'It would never work,' she said.

'I know,' he confirmed.

'And now is too late, no?' She wasn't asking him, just underlining the state of play.

'It is,' he said.

Milduta lowered her eyes, as if already accepting her fate.

61

She stood in silence just inches away from him, her gaze directed at the damp wooden floor of the ship's deck.

Jack raised his arm and suddenly pushed her.

Milduta offered no resistance.

Her body toppled over the rail and disappeared into the darkness and the sea. The sound of her limp body hitting the surface below was lost amongst the other ambient noises filtering from all corners of the boat, as it raced towards the coast.

He knew from a past conversation that Milduta could not swim.

Jack looked at the illuminated face of his Tag Heuer: it was almost one in the morning. A Sunday.

A wave of terrible tiredness suddenly gripped Jack and he made his way back to his cabin. He knew he would sleep for a very long time.

The distant horizon lay 200 miles off both the coasts of Denmark and Germany.

Also by Maxim Jakubowski published by THE DO-NOT PRESS

Life In The World Of Women

A collection of vile, dangerous and loving stories...

ISBN: 1 899344 06 3 paperback (£6.99)

Maxim Jakubowski's dangerous and erotic stories of war between the sexes are collected here for the first time, together with three major new pieces. Inter-linked themes and characters run through the nine stories as the work comes together episode by episode before reaching a bloody climax in a New Orleans brothel.

Taking in aspects of crime noir, erotica, romance and gritty social drama, *Life In The World Of Women* reflects a world where sexual appetites are unusual and insatiable, where morals take a back seat and where passions run high. It is a world where death can be as close as the next meal, and where uncertainty is the only sure thing.

Also by Maxim Jakubowski published by THE DO-NOT PRESS

The State of Montana

Daring, touching, frightening; The State of Montana is Maxim Jakubowski at his erotic best.

ISBN: 1-899344-43-8   paperback (£5.00)

A challenging erotic novel from the man who has been called 'The King of the Erotic Thriller' – but this time the thrills are of a different nature…

Montana has never been to Montana but often dreams of its open skies and chilly valleys. Montana is the name Adrienne selected from childhood movie memories for her Internet handle.

The EROTIC Novels
Limited Edition Boxed Set

It's You That I Want To Kiss
Because She Thought She Loved Me
On Tenderness Express
+ unique 16-page signed & numbered booklet

ISBN: 1-899344-80-2   Limited Edition Boxed Set (£12.99)

'An unholy mixture of Jim Thomspson and American Pyscho'
Time Out

Adventure, mystery and sex-on-the road are at the heart of the volumes featured in this signed, numbered limited edition (250) box set by the 'King of the erotic thriller' (*Crime Time*).

In *It's You That I Want To Kiss* jacob and Anne meet – and full in lust – in Miami Beach. But their tryst takes a dangerous turn when Anne accepts a courier job to Cracas and ends up with a fortune in stolen diamonds. In *Because She Thought She Loved Me*, Joe falls hard for Caitleen, his boss' wife, and the two scheme to kill her clueless husband in the perfect crime. But Joe doesn't count in Caitleen's bizarre sexual appetites…

In *On Tenderness Express*, hard-bitten detective Martin Jackson and his exotically beautiful client, Cornelia, pose as a pair of dominant-submissives in order to crack a case.

This prestigious boxed set of critically-acclaimed 'naked noir' (*Kirkus Reviews*) is priced at £9.50 lower than the collective published price and comes with an exclusive 16-page introduction booklet, each one signed and numbered by the author.

'Hard-boiled, proudly pornographic thriller…'
The Literary Review

Also published by THE DO-NOT PRESS

Pick Any Title
by Russell James

RUSSELL JAMES is Chairman of the CRIME WRITERS' ASSOCIATION 2001-2002

PICK ANY TITLE is a magnificent new crime caper involving sex, humour sudden death and double-cross.

'Lord Clive' bought his lordship at a 'Lord of the Manor' sale where titles fetch anything from two to two hundred thousand pounds. Why not buy another cheap and sell it high? Why stop at only one customer? Clive leaves the beautiful Jane Strachey to handle his American buyers, each of whom imagines himself a lord.

But Clive was careless who he sold to, and among his victims are a shrewd businessman, a hell-fire preacher and a vicious New York gangster. When lawyers pounce and guns slide from their holsters Strachey finds she needs more than good looks and a silver tongue to save her life.

A brilliant page-turner from 'the best of Britain's darker crime writers'
The Times

Also published by THE DO-NOT PRESS

First of the True Believers by Paul Charles

'The Autobiography of Theodore Hennessy'

ISBN 1899344 78 0 paperback (£7.50)
ISBN 1899344 79 9 hardcover (£15.00)

THE BEATLES formed in 1959 and became the biggest group in the world. Among other less celebrated Merseybeat groups of the time were The Nighttime Passengers, led by Theo Hennessy, who almost replaced Pete Best as drummer of the 'Fab Four'.

First of The True Believers tells of a decade in the life of Theodore Hennessy, intertwined with the story of The Beatles. It begins in 1959 with his first meeting with the beautiful and elusive Marianne Burgess and follows their subsequent on-off love affair and his rise as a musician.

The Beatles provided the definitive soundtrack to the '60s, and here novelist and musicologist Paul Charles combines their phenomenal story with a tender-hearted tale of sex, love and rock 'n' roll in '60s Liverpool.

Also published by THE DO-NOT PRESS

Mr Romance
by Miles Gibson

The new novel: an epic tale of love, lust, jealousy, pain
and purple prose

ISBN 1899344 89 6   paperback (£6.99)
ISBN 1899344 90 X   hardcover (£15.00)

'Miles Gibson is a natural born poet'
Ray Bradbury

Skipper shares his parents' boarding house with their lodgers:
lovely Janet the bijou beauty and Senor Franklin, the volcanic
literary genius. Life is sweet, until one night the lugubrious Mr
Marvel seeks shelter with them.

Who is the mysterious fugitive and what dark secret haunts
him? Skipper sets out to solve the riddle. But then the astonishing Dorothy Clark arrives and his life is thrown into turmoil.
Skipper falls hopelessly in love and plans a grand seduction.
He'll stop at nothing. But Dorothy is saving herself for Jesus…

Also published by THE DO-NOT PRESS

Double Take
by Mike Ripley

Double Take: The novel and the screenplay (the funniest caper movie never made) in a single added-value volume.

ISBN 1899344 81 0 paperback (£6.99)
ISBN 1899344 82 9 hardcover (£15.00)

Double Take tells how to rob Heathrow and get away with it (enlist the help of the police). An 'Italian Job' for the 21st century, with bad language – some of it translated – chillis as offensive weapons, but no Minis. It also deconstructs one of Agatha Christie's most audacious plots.

The first hilarious stand-alone novel from the creator of the best-selling Angel series.